PIRU LOVE
PART 2

Kre Kre

Please join us on the following Social Networks:
www.kalikrepublications.com
www.facebook.com/kalikrepublications
kalikre@gmail.com
Blog: http://kalikre.wordpress.com/

PIRU (pīe-roo) n. 1. A Blood Gang originated in Compton, California, in the early 70's. 2. A street that starts in Los Angeles, East of San Pedro Street and ends at South Mona Blvd in Compton. 3. A person who identifies themselves as an affiliate of a group that wears burgundy, or red attire.

LOVE (luv) n. 1. A deep and tender feeling of affection for attachment or devotion to a person or persons. 2. A feeling of brotherhood and good will toward other people. 3. Strong liking for or interest in something.

ONE

October 31, 1989   Monday 8:35 p.m.

"Trick or Treat smell my feet give me something good to eat!" yelled a group of children in unison. Deena opened the door to her mother's residence dressed in all black as a witch, with a huge bowl of candy in her hand. She grabbed handful after handful of treats and divided it amongst the children evenly. The kids were thankful of the bite sized Snickers, Chick-o-sticks, Lemonheads, Big Blo's, Twix's, Boston baked beans, Cherry Chans and Blow pops that she dished out not being stingy. "Thank you wicked witch!"

"You welcome honey!" Deena responded, as she watched the group flee from her porch through the yard and out the front gate. She looked down the street on both ends of the block, to see if any more kids were nearby. The block was clear. Deena turned off the porch light and grabbed her broom and plastic jack-o-lantern candy bucket that was filled with candy and a loaded .380 automatic handgun. She slid the mini-broom through the plastic strap handle that was attached to the candy bucket, grabbed the orange skateboard that's against the fence inside of the yard and exited the yard, closing the fence behind her. She contemplated on which direction she was gonna take first before moving. Moments later, she dropped the skateboard onto the ground and pushed east on 129th street in route to the Compton Watts area.

*****

It took Deena longer than usual to get to this area on Central Boulevard and 120th street. She stops her skateboard alongside of a parked car to straighten out her Halloween costume. She uses the window on a 1976 Chevy Caprice as a mirror. Her face is covered with white make-up, while the wells of both of her eyes are covered with black make-up, giving Deena a dark gothic look. She takes a pair of black nylon gloves from out of the pumpkin and places them on. She checks her hat, pulling it down firmly onto her head. Then adjusts her black gown, before she walks over to Taco Pete on the corner and waits for a victim to knock down.

Taco Pete is a well-known and one of the most dangerous food stands in the greater Los Angeles County. The side of the street that it does business on, is claimed by the 120th street Miller Gangsters. A well-known Blood gang known for bank robbing and killing rival Crips such as: The 8 ball Crips, Mc Kinley Crips, 116th Street Kitchen Crips and The Carver Park Crips. Over the years, gang members from both sides of the color barrier come here to get food, only to leave the scene in a coroner's van.

Deena posts in between two parked cars in the parking lot out the way and view of patrons buying grub. She checks her wrist watch for the time, it reads 9:35 p.m. Customized cars and trucks zoom north and south on Central boulevard pounding Rap music, while cars driving east and west on 120th street does the same. However, none turns into the lot. The plot thickens.

Thirty minutes have rolled by and Deena's ass cheeks are falling asleep, due to her sitting on the parking lot length, wooden stall that stops cars from hitting the brick wall. She stood up shaking her legs and jiggling her ass cheeks back to life. Across the street is a known liquor store that the 8 Ball and Carver Park Crips claim. A starburst blue 1977 Monte Carlo, sitting on lace rims and vogue tires pulls into the parking lot blasting 'Me, myself and I,' by De La Soul.

Three Crips climb out of the hooptie, dressed in blue khakis and white T-shirts. Two Crips stroll toward the liquor store, while the other one tells the two Crips that he's going across the street to Taco Pete. They all nod in agreement.

Deena nipples become erect at the sight of her potential victim. She squints, adjusting her vision as the Crip bells across Central Boulevard, pulling bills from both of his front khaki pockets. As he gets in front of Taco Pete's order window, he quickly looks above checking the menu. Deena's heart beats in overtime once she notices her half-brother Maurice. She knew if she killed him, China would be free from captivity. She quickly reached into her plastic pumpkin, grabbing the pistol and putting one in the chamber. She dusted all the particles off the skateboard, so that her shoe would get a firm grip on the board. Right before she was about to skate past him shooting, he bounced side to side lifting each leg, signifying that he had to piss. So deena waited, watching him with an eagle's eye for him to slip up. After he placed his order, he swiftly walked deep into the dark parking lot whipping out his cheesy dick and pissing onto the brick wall, turning from side to side, as if his cock is an assault rifle and he's gunning down his rivals.

Deena had to time this mission with precision, cause if she doesn't kill him, she could be her mother's cell mate.

His urinalysis came to an end. He bounced up and down on the arch of his blue suede pumas, while tucking his pecker back into his boxers.

"Hey Maurice!" yelled one of his Crip comrades from across the street at the liquor store's parking lot.

"Fuck!" Deena mumbled, at the sight of the other two Crips across the street. She is now pressed for time and must decide fast. The Crips at the liquor store stay posted smoking on a Newport cigarette and gulping down a 40 ounce of Olde English 800 beer.

Maurice slowly walks from the brick wall through the dark parking lot. "I was pissing cuz, hold up!"

Deena watched him through the booger stained window of a 1986, 5.0 GT Mustang that belongs to one of the workers inside of Taco Pete. On time, she zoomed from in between the two cars on her skateboard like a witch riding on her broom on a mission. Maurice was walking with his head down, until he heard the wheels of a skateboard heading towards him, pushing through the parking lot with force. Before he could utter one word, he saw a flash of light, followed by a sound of firecrackers popping rapidly. His lifeless body slammed onto the pavement of the lot hard.

"Cuz! Cuz! The homie getting shot!" the two Crips screamed, panicking out of control as they nervously jumped back into the Monte Carlo.

Deena stopped the skateboard and put two more slugs in the back of her brother's head, making sure that he is now a Crip ghost. She picked up her skateboard, then walked several feet down 120th street, turning into the back part of what is known as, The Ujima Village area; but is also known as the Willow brook area. This is the home of the Village Town Pirus. Cars are unable to enter the housing projects from this side. She is aware of that, so she kept walking until she disappeared into thin air.

TWO

November 1, 1989   Tuesday 12:02 p.m.

Solomon flicks through the various channels on his television and cable box. He stops at the channel five local news, KTLA and turns up the volume. He strolls from the living room into the kitchen and pours himself a mixing bowl full of Golden Grahams, mixing it with Minute Maid orange juice. He overheard the reporter talking live to the Chief of Police, about all the different gang style slayings that took place last night throughout the greater Los Angeles area and county. Solomon hurries back into the living room, to catch the latest and the greatest.

Solomon becomes numb when a photo of Maurice appears onto the screen and the footage of a body covered up with a white sheet, behind Taco Pete taped off with yellow tape.

"Damn that's crazy," Solomon mumbled

underneath his breath.

An eight month pregnant Christina wobbles through the living room, in route to the kitchen to stuff her pie hole with food items that don't mix. Her favorite was crunched up Cheetos and bacon bits, sprinkled on top of melted pralines and cream ice cream; chasing it with a cup of garlic coffee.

"Honey what are you doing?" she asked, gathering up the items to make her favorite concoction.

"Man, I was just sitting here tripping off the news. They found my step brother dead behind Taco Pete last night," Solomon expressed, not really showing any sympathy.

"Oh my, honey are you serious?" Christina asked out of concern, walking into the living room to console her man.

Solomon began chuckling.

"Why are you laughing honey?" That's not a

laughing matter, or is it?" Christina asked confused.

"Well, he's the clown that came to my mother's house on his father's birthday, dressed in all blue disrespecting. After the family put hands and feet on his ass and shot at him; my brother Kyle was murdered in front of the house afterwards. So, my mother assumed that he did it and tried to kill him but missed. They arrested my mother for the attempt on him and a murder on his homeboy. But the crazy part is he was the star witness. But he's dead now. So, no witness no case," Solomon explained nodding in agreement. "We'll be hearing from my mother in about a week or two."

"Oh, I see. Well, what do you have planned for today?"

"Nothing important, I'mma go and check on both of my properties, then check on my sisters and homeboys. Why? You need for me to take you somewhere?" Solomon asked out of curiosity. He didn't need to be sidetracked or slowed down.

"No babe, I'm good. I'm in the house all day. I'm going to watch my stories and get some rest. Your son and daughter is beating me up," she expressed smiling, rubbing her stomach. "Babe, why don't you take my car instead of driving yours. I don't want anything to happen to you babe."

"Okay, I'll roll the Benzo," he shot back, smiling at Christina. He watched as Christina slowly walked back into the bedroom. He reminisced on the first day that he and Christina met in the classroom and how she used to watch him closely. To see her waddle back into their bedroom, was a major accomplishment. On top of that, he snatched her from the sucka ass cop that smoked Big Chinadog. Now she has two young Pirus in the oven. God is good.

*****

Solomon gets off on the Imperial Highway exit turning right, then making another turn onto Figueroa

Street heading south. Moments later, he slows down and makes a right turn onto 119th street. He pulls into the driveway of a dark pink stucco decorated, three-bedroom home that's vacant. This is a newly purchased tax credit home that he bought and fixed up. This home would be ready to rent out as soon as he gets installation installed in the attic. This make Solomon's third home that he owns and rents out. He steps out of the Benz with an extra set of keys that belongs to the house. Solomon glances at his stainless steel and gold men's Rolex watch, which reads 2:35 p.m. He had plenty of time to give the rental a once over. He walked in leaving the door ajar, as he went into the kitchen checking the cabinets and sink; then into the laundry area. This rental property is located between Denver street and Figueroa, an area that is claimed by the West side, One twenty Denver Lanes. So, he wasn't tripping off any unexpected visitors. Plus, he knew eighty percent of the gang bangers over here. He walks into the bathroom flushing the toilet, to see if it still works. Like new money, the toilet did its thing. Solomon whipped out and pissed in the toilet. While whizzing, Solomon can hear another vehicle pulling into the driveway. But whoever it was, sounded like they were in a rush or something. He tilted his ear towards the window of the bathroom, to see if he could hear more. He couldn't, so he shook his dick vigorously of all its pissy contents and placed his gun back into its holster and zipped up. He quickly washed off his hands with plain water, looking around the bathroom for something to dry his dick beaters off with. He finds nothing, so he fans his hands in the air while walking through the hallway in route to the living room.

CLICK.

From the side of his face, he can see the barrel of a 10-millimeter handgun, trembling. "You little son-of-a-bitch. I should blow your fucking head off punk!"

Solomon tries to turn slowly to the side to see his

aggressor, but the female won't let him. She demands through a set of clenched teeth. "You little slimy muthafucka, you're gonna pay. You think that you can just fuck me and leave me hanging? Huh, answer me you little sexy bitch!"

Solomon recognizes the voice. This is the same psychotic bitch that tried to smoke him in the hospital that night. His mind is racing of a technique to disarm this looney bitch. "Ms. Crutchfield babe, what's wrong? Why are you tripping? Why don't you talk to me, so we can resolve this matter?"

"Pull your pants down," she ordered, pushing him in the jaw with the handgun. "Now!"

"Huh? You want me to pull my pants down? For what babe? I don't understand," Solomon asked confused. But at the same time, he wasn't trying to get shot either. So, he slowly unbuckled his belt.

"I'm shooting you in the dick nigga, watch. Watch me muthafucka!" she shouted, as she slowly walked in front of him, looking at him face to face breathing heavily. "You saw me looking at your muthafucking ass through the window that day. But what did you do? You went over there to your little Piru homeboys and made fun of me huh? Didn't you? Did you tell them that I was pregnant you muthafucka? Huh?"

Solomon's heart fell into his shoe. The thought alone of getting this looney bitch pregnant, made the hairs on his back stand up. But he had to use his charm to seduce her. "Baby that's good news, that's wonderful. Did you keep the baby?"

Ms. Crutchfield answered sobbing heavily, with tears streaming down both sides of her cheek. "Yes, we have a daughter. She is so beautiful. Her name is April, she's eight months old."

She removed the gun from Solomon's face. He hugs her tight to console her.

"I didn't know Ms. Crutchfield. I apologize, I never meant to hurt you. This is all new to me, you're my baby momma," Solomon replied proudly, trying to cheer her up. "I wanna see my daughter, this is my first child."

That statement alone put a pep back in Ms. Crutchfield's step. "Call me Sara babe."

Solomon's charm worked. She bit like a big mouth bass. Now it's time to lay it on thick. "Baby I wanna see my daughter. I wanna give her a kiss and take pictures with her."

Ms. Crutchfield wasn't trying to hear all that frivolous conversation. She tossed the pistol onto the carpet, kneeled in front of Solomon's crotch, pulled his pants down to his ankles and slowly shoved his wood into her filthy mouth, sucking his cock hard. Sara served him so good, that he stood on his tippy toes while grabbing the back of her head, fucking her face like a real champion. Sara loved every minute of it. The reason why she had an attitude in the first place, is because no so-called man doesn't handle her like the slut that she really is and wants to be. This is why she's deeply in love with your boy Solo. He talks major shit to her, then backs it up with a dick lashing.

"Hold on," Solomon explained, taking off all his clothes. He quickly ran to the front door securing it, because he knows she's about to get loud.

Sara follows suit by snatching off all her clothing also, lying on her back with her knees touching her breast. Solomon walked over to her and pinned her knees to her chest and began stabbing her pussy with major pressure, as if he was killing some Crips with a knife.

"Bitch, you've been acting up huh?" Solomon asked, while shoving his cock from the tip to the nuts inside of her funk fest with force.

"Yes daddy, Yes!" she shouted, falling back deeply in love with Solomon. "I've been showing my black ass baby, spank me!"

Like a soldier taking a command from his

lieutenant. He began pounding faster. Her pussy got so wet, all you heard was splashing sounds. He turned her on her knees like a dog and went HAM (HARD AS A MUTHAFUCKA).

"Do you like it like this, you crazy ass bitch?" Solomon asked, pulling her micro mini braids by the base, yanking it, while his nuts slap the back of her pussy, making her extra wet. "Answer me, you crazy ass bitch! Do you like it?"

"Yes daddy, yes. I'm a crazy bitch, punish me," she begged truthfully, loving her baby daddy's filthy mouth.

"Here, taste your sweet pussy bitch," Solomon responded, acting a fool. He pulled out of her pussy and pushed her onto the carpet face up. He stood over her already opened mouth and slowly lowered his dick into her mouth, with his right hand. Sara power sucked his cock until she gagged for air.

The two went at it until they suffered from severe

carpet burns. Sara got the fix that she needed, now she can function like a tax paying citizen again. Because prior to this dick down that she just received, she was flashing on any and everybody and didn't give a shit as to who were in their feelings. Fuck em and feed em fish.

After they got dressed, Solomon hugged her from behind, kissing her neck and earlobe occasionally.

"When can I see my daughter? We're gonna have to meet up because I live…."

"I already know baby, "Sara interrupted cutting him off. "I know where you live, who you live with, when the twins are due and everybody that's trying to do you."

Solomon heart rate sped up. "You know everything about me baby momma?"

"Everything, even that birth mark that's on your left ankle," Sara explained indirectly letting him know he better not get out of pocket. "I'm that other grey Crown

Vic that you saw that day, trailing behind the police that shot you up that night."

Solomon pooted out of nervousness. He let her go and pulled the sheet back from the front window, to get a view of the grey Crown Vic that is parked on the front lawn sideways. Solomon formed a lump in his throat. Because on the for real, he's slipping like a muthafucka. He's a street nigga no doubt, but the industry lifestyle is the life he would rather live. So, he know it's wise to keep this lunatic bitch in his corner. He already knows that everybody and their mama is hating, so it's time to play chess.

"Baby momma, we have to figure out a schedule, so that I can give you your weekly or monthly fix, because I don't need or want any problems where I live. And that's out of respect for baby mama number two," Solomon explained keeping it way real.

"I'll call you every two weeks or better yet, just come to my house on the 1st and 15th of every month.

That way you can see your daughter and feel this pussy all in the same day." Sara expressed flashing a warm smile. She respected him for keeping it real and not lying to her trying to be sneaky, like most youngsters his age would've done. "I respect the fact that you didn't deceive me just now baby daddy. Just keep it one hundred with your baby momma number one at all times and you won't have any problems out of me. Okay?"

"You got that, that's how I get down anyway," he responded, adjusting his clothing looking around the house, seeing if he left anything behind. He points towards her Roscoe (pistol) letting her know, to not leave that behind. He doesn't need a case right now, life is too good.

His baby momma retrieves the jammy (gun) and puts it in her waist behind her back. She gives her baby daddy a long passionate kiss, before she departs. "Oh, and don't worry yourself about that other Crown Vic.

I'm going to put somebody on that pig's helmet, now that you accept me as your baby mama. Because if you would've denied me or our baby, you would've been ten toes up right now and I would've been in route to Baldwin Hills right now to finish everybody off."

"Thank God I'm a real nigga with sense huh?" Solomon replied, rubbing the bottom of his chin in thought.

Sara walked out of the house, pecking him on the cheek, as she sashays off the porch. "I love you Solomon, take care of yourself. I'll contact you first, then we'll go from there."

"I love you more baby mama," he responded, watching her climb into the Crown Vic, mashing west on 119th street getting in the wind. Solomon locks the front door to his property and heads to the block.

*****

Deena sits in the living room of her mother's

home bored to death. She's been holding down the home thanks to her grandmother, Solomon and the big homie Nine. She is sipping on a cup of Hennessey and coke, listening to *I Like,* by Guy. She hears the honking of a car horn, so she walks to the front door that's open and watch as Solomon gets out of the car, through the bar door. Deena sits back down with an attitude.

"Hey Deena," he called, putting both hands on the bars trying to peek in.

"Come in!" Deena shouted, rolling her eyes at him. She turned down the stereo a few notches. "I said come in!"

He heard the attitude in her voice and already knew what time it was. But he wasn't going for it, not even a little bit. He had a look of seriousness on his face as he entered. "Blood what's happening?"

Deena shook her head with her lip turned up "Just bicking it blood, sipping on some drank that's all, listening to the stereo. Ain't shit popping around here.

23

Niggas doing movies and shit."

Solomon shook his head chuckling, as he sat in the recliner chair by the door. "Blood, I saw Maurice's picture this morning, he got laid down last night."

"Yeah, I know all about it. Fuck that nigga, this Piru. Now our mother should be home on her next court date. I mean shit, ain't no more witnesses," Deena explained, not showing any remorse to their step brother turned Crip.

"Where Sabrina at?"

"Across the street with granny. I stay over here alone. Me, myself and I," Deena shot back, still with an attitude. She takes two more sips of the Hennessey, then places the cup on the coffee table."

"What's with the attitude blood? Did I do something to you my nigga," Solomon asked, adjusting his Pittsburgh Pirates cap firmly on his dome. Soon after crossing his legs, resting both hands on top of his knees.

"That's the problem my nigga. You ain't doing me," she shot back serious.

"Come on now blood. I thought we grew out of that stage and left those skeletons behind us," Solomon replied, not feeling Deena right now one bit. On the low, she's starting to get on bloods bad side pressing him for dick.

"What? I gotta be a white woman? I don't have enough money?" Deena asked, slurring out her words from being tipsy.

Solomon shook his head out of disgust, as he looked throughout the living room and kitchen, playing it off. Deena is making her brother uncomfortable. "Now you know that doesn't have nothing to do with it. You done got drunk and opened up them portals, letting those evil spirits in."

She stood onto her feet drunk and unbalanced, ripping open her white button down Guess shirt, exposing her voluptuous bra-less, brown juicy firm titties. She stumbles around the coffee table and falls onto her brothers lap hella drunk, pulling her pants down by the waist, exposing the top of her nappy headed pussy hairs. Solomon forms a bulge in his pants so hard, that his asshole tightens up, like it was covered with crazy glue. Solomon is trying hard to fight this sexual demon, but the demon is winning.

"Take me in the room and fuck me, you know you want to," the demon spoke out of Deena. She pulled her pants down below her hot moist smelling pussy, that had an aroma of hot ejaculated semen.

Solomon mind was racing. He was damned if he did, and damned if he didn't. He picked his sister up and carried her into the bedroom and laid her down into the bed softly. He watched in awe as his sister somehow came back to life, stripping down until she was in the nude. She fell onto her back with her legs spread eagle, shoving two fingers inside of her pussy, then into her mouth, slowly sucking the sauce off of them.

"Let me lock the front door, so that we won't get caught," Solomon explained, grabbing his boner through his pants.

"Okay hurry," Deena responded super horny and ready to get it on.

Solomon turned off the light in the living room then stepped out, locking the door behind him and softly closing the bar door shut. He jogged through the front yard, jumped in the car and smashed out. That bitch was tripping on bloods. He wasn't going to fall for the banana in the tail pipe.

THREE

November 23, 1989   Wednesday 12:35 p.m.

     Chinadoll's front yard was packed, with gang members from various Blood neighborhoods, throughout the greater Los Angeles, Compton, Watts and Inglewood areas. Her case was dropped by the D.A. due to technicalities within the witnesses. The time she spent in the county jail fighting her case, took its toll on her. She put on a few extra pounds, especially around the hip, thighs and ass area of her body. Her hair was longer and her skin complexion had her looking pale as a ghost. She is in dying need of some California sun and some hard dick. All she thought about while she was locked down was getting piped down. Since Chinadog's death, nobody penetrated those sugar walls. Dike bitches pushed up on China trying to put a tongue to her kitty kat, but to no avail, China is strictly dickly. She let them hoes know that, she wasn't even gay for the stay.

Every sibling from China's immediate family was present except for Solomon. Ever since Deena pulled that stunt with him that night, he hasn't been showing his face much.

"Momma, are you going to cook for Thanksgiving?" Deena asked, taking a sip from her red plastic cup filled with Hennessey and coke.

China scratched her head in thought. "Um, sure, we can cook something, why not?"

"Okay," Deena replied, in route to the kitchen, pulling out all of the utensils that she needs to get Thanksgiving on and popping.

While everyone was smoking and drinking in the front yard. No one paid attention to the gray Crown Victoria that slid by. The car stood at the stop sign on a 129th street and Towne Avenue, longer than usual, like the occupants of the car was scoping out the scene. The back window came down slowly, stopping halfway. Then the barrel of a street sweeper twelve gage, eased out the window, slowly letting off three rounds. Everybody scattered in different directions. Some members immediately hit the ground, while others hid behind cars, and trash cans that were out front. When the firing stopped, a few Pirus returned fire, letting them fools in the Crown Vic know, it ain't that type of party. The Crown Vic smashed off west on 129th street. Three Bloods ran into the middle of the street, letting the vehicle have it. The Crown Vic swerved out of control, until it reached San Pedro Street, making a left turn getting somewhere.

China stormed out of her home, into the front yard with pistol in hand heated. "Blood, what kind of car was that?" she asked, to no one in particular.

All three of the Pirus that were in the street, ran over to the front gate entrance, meeting China there.

"It was a gray Crown Vic Blood," responded one of the gun men breathing heavily.

"Fuck! I haven't been home one day and these

muthafucka's is already with the bullshit," China vented shaking her head in disbelief. China shoved her pistol in her right front pocket. "Is everybody cool Blood?"

"Yeah Big Homie," someone from the pack responded. China would've lost it, if one of the homies had gotten hit.

Everyone that was on the ground got up dusting themselves off from the grass that were stuck to their clothing. Piru members who left their pistols in the car the first time went and got them and put them into their front right pants pocket. Let somebody else come through popping, they vowed to flip their asses on the next go around.

A 1977, orange four door Chevy Nova pulls in front of China's residence, stopping in the middle of the street. Smurf, Kay Kay, Vanity and Tina-Ru climb out of the vehicle pumped. They left the vehicle in the middle of the street on purpose, to slow the traffic down just in case anybody else get any bright ideas. All four females are strapped with handguns sticking out from their front pants pocket, letting it be known that they are armed and dangerous.

The shooting was heard throughout the area. Cars started pulling up from every direction, with members from Athens Park, Miller Gangsters and the C.J.C. Mafia. This is another faction of the Rolling One Thirty Pirus, that also claim Athens Park, (Cook, Jarvis, Carlton).

Smurf jumped back into the Nova and parked down the street, so that the rest of the Blood homies can find some space to park their cars and party.

A white convertible K-5 blazer pulls up slowly, pounding *Whodini's*, Freaks come out at night. The four occupants inside nod their heads to the beat and acknowledges everyone in the front by flashing gang signs. This is Ru-Zell, Fat-Fat, G-Rabb and Big Herm. They see a parking space by Jefty's Restaurant and park, to join China-Ru's party. What started as a welcome home party, is slowly building up to a block party. China is loving every minute of it too.

"China-Ru!" Tina-Ru playfully shouted, walking up to her big homie, giving her a long hug. She pulled back to examine China's curvaceous body. "Blood, how you doing?"

"Shit better than most," China responded, popping slick, cupping her breast with both hands flossing her new body on Tina-Ru. They both chuckle. Tina-Ru wasn't gay, but she started halfway feigning on the big homies body.

"I see you... that's from all them zoom zoom and wham wham," Tina replied, joking.

"So what's up blood, put me up on the latest and greatest," China shot back on a serious note. They both walk through the front yard, past the driveway and house to the backyard. The backyard is unoccupied. China leans up against the side of the garage, shoving a Newport in between her lips, lighting it. Tina-Ru stack up two crates making a chair in front of China, so they can talk.

"Blood, peep the script ...you're about to be a grandmother, twice," explained Tina-Ru, rolling her eyes at the thought.

"Twice? She's having twins?" China asked, excitedly, blowing smoke through her nose. She smiled at the thought, of being a gang banging granny.

"Yeah, she should be having them within the next month she's about eight months prego," Tina explained, frowning, thinking that Solomon was dead wrong getting their teacher knocked up. She thought Solo was going to do her, like what he had done to her. Sex her real good, then shake her by going back to the block to hang with the homies. However, she was wrong.

China was stuck in a trance, in deep thought. She took one more drag from the Port, then put it out against the garage, exhaling. She had to make the right decision, because once she makes a call, its final. So she didn't want any mistakes allowed. "Damn, that boy is growing up fast."

Your son is having money. You should see that big ass house they're living in. She don't even teach at Centennial anymore, that's how much dough they have. You know she's white or Italian so they know how to invest and flip their money, because you already know, if that was a black woman that he was with, they would've been in Hawthorne or Inglewood in a one bedroom apartment. He don't even come around, he's that busy," Tina-Ru explained, laying it on kind of thick telling China what she think she wants to hear.

She came to your spot to holler at you?" Tina-Ru asked surprised, adjusting the pistol in her front pocket.

China nodded in agreement. "Yeah, when he was locked up. She parked, got out the car and walked into this front yard."

"She wasn't scared?" Tina asked sounding a little foolish.

"Shit, scared of what?" China asked, with a confused look on her face.

"Shit, white folks are scared to come to the hood, except for the police," she responded, trying to convince China.

China shook her head disagreeing with Tina's statement. "Well, she wasn't scared one bit. To keep it way real, I have respect for her."

Deep in the back of Tina's mind, she knew she was really wasting her time trying to harm Christina. Because killing her is not going to make him love her or better yet, want to be with her. If anything, it would piss Solomon off and make him convert to his old ways; gang banging. Tina looked up to China and respected her call as a big homie; but she and Christina's husband made a pact, so she had to follow through. Because at the end of the day, it all boils down to the money. So, if she had to choose between climbing the financial ladder or Christina's life; Christina needs to go out and buy a black dress, because she's out of here. But what they're unaware of is baby mama number one, who has Solomon's back to the death of her.

"I feel you on that big homie," Tina-Ru lied, but kept the conversation going to pass time.

"Just make sure the timing is right, so that I can personally put one in that cocksucker dome. The night they were supposed to take China to jail; that pig looked me straight in the eye and lied to my face. They knew he was *shermed* out and took it personally when he ran from them, so now it's personal with me and that son-of-a-bitch." China responded with conviction, firing up another cigarette, adjusting her pistol in her pocket. "And on a more personal note, Solomon's father found me and sent me fifteen hundred dollars. So we started corresponding with each other. In every letter he asked about Solomon and wanted his information so that he can get to know his son. I didn't tell him that he is starting to be a famous filmmaker."

"China-Ru!" yelled Mama-Ru, walking through the driveway, making her way to the backyard. "China blood, where you at?"

China recognizes the voice and becomes excited. "Blood, we back here!" Mama-Ru, is another well-known Piru member from 142nd street in Compton. She runs up on China giving her a long hug rocking from side to side.

"Blood, they finally let you out of there huh?" Mama-Ru asked, pulling back from China taking a glance at her new figure.

"On Piru, it was about fucking time. I was starting to get fat up in there," China responded laughing, thumping the remainder of her cigarette in the grass.

Mama walked over to Tina-Ru and gave her a hug. "What's up tina blood? What you doing?"

"I ain't doing shit, just chopping it up with China. How you doing big homie?" Tina-Ru asked.

"Man I'm doing fair for a square. I just came to

pay my respect, I heard the homie was out," Mama-Ru explained, with a smile on her face.

"That's what's up," China and Tina responded in unison.

"Alright, I'mma let y'all finish hollering blood, be up," said Mama-Ru as she walked back through the driveway, in route to the front yard.

"Alright homie," Tina-Ru responded, as she stood up stretching. She motioned to China, that she wanted to head back to the party to get her drink, smoke and conversation on with other homies that's in the front yard hanging. China trails behind her young homie.

The rest of the day, the welcoming home function had no other problems since the shooting occurred. On the low, China was trying to throw the pussy on a few of her young homies, but they declined out of love and respect. That was starting to piss her off, because she was long overdue for a tune up. She had to find an outlet. Solomon's father was the only person that she can call to get some swipe. Desperate times calls for desperate measures.

*****

Solomon walked into an auditorium that was filled to its maximum capacity, with students, teachers, news reporters and scholars from around the world. He's a guest speaker tonight at the University of Southern California. He strolled to the podium dressed in red clothing from head to toe. He removed his Pittsburgh Pirates, fitted baseball cap, exposing his freshly twisted French braids that hangs down his back and shoulders.

"Good evening ladies and gentlemen. My name is Solomon Spencer, better known as Solo. I am a non-active member of the Rolling 130 Pirus, in the greater Los Angeles/Compton area. I am responsible for the independent film: 'The Lifestyle of a Piru Gang member.' As of now, I am under the tutelage of the infamous Barry Burris. My next project is a full-length film, titled 'Piru

Love.' Does anyone have any questions?" asked Solomon, looking out at the sea of people. An elderly white woman, somewhere in her early sixties raised her hand. "Yes, what is your question ma'am?"

The woman stands up. "Mr. Spencer, where do you see yourself in the next five years, as a film maker."

Solomon pondered on her question, rubbing his chin grinning. "In the next five years, I see myself with two hit movies and an Oscar under my belt."

Everyone in the auditorium laughed.

A tall Asian man raises his hand. Solomon acknowledges him. He stands up. "Mr. Spencer, I watched your documentary when it was in West Hollywood at the Sundance film festival. First and foremost, I would like to say that you did an outstanding job, as far as, helping me understand why individuals join gangs. Every member was very articulate and straight to the point, great job."

Solomon nodded his head at the Asian man. "Thank you, sir. I appreciate you going out and supporting my film. It's an honor. I'm blessed thank You."

Solomon answered everyone's question in the audience. He captivated the crowd with his charm, good attitude and great mannerism. Afterwards, he signed autographs and took pictures with who-ever. He removed the stigma that was once attached to gang members. Solomon was approachable. Women thought he was very handsome and easy on the eyes. They would touch his hair in awe, captivated by his presence.

Terry was also present, he quickly navigated through the sea of fans, in route to tell Solomon the news that they've been waiting to hear. "Solomon!"

Solomon turned around noticing Terry, who was waving his hand, telling him to come to him. Solomon knew it must have been important, so he hugged and shook the hands of his fans as he departed. Terry meets him halfway, giving him the good news. Solomon and Terry high five each other and hug. The documentary was picked up by H.B.O. Now the world can watch his work as a producer, actor and film maker right from their living rooms. The window of opportunity is wide open. God is good.

FOUR

May 10, 1992   Thursday 11:35 a.m.

Three years later

Solomon and Christina gave birth to a set of beautiful twins. Eve and Day. They were named by the way they were born. Eve, the girl came out first on Christmas Eve at approximately 11:57 p.m. Then Day, the boy came out three minutes later at midnight on the nose on Christmas day. These twins are descendants from Satan himself. All day they cause havoc, moving on their own agenda. The only way Solomon and Christina can handle them is when they are promised the three M's: Money, Music and Mc Donald's. Christina lets them run over her because she feels that in a couple of years they will grow out of it. On the other hand, Solomon occasionally whoops them with a belt or puts them on punishment from one; if not all the M's. Solomon babysits most of the time during the day, while Christina overseas their business ventures. The twins always seem to embarrass her when she takes them out in public, that's why she leaves them with their dad.

Solomon's first child by Sara, is only nine months older than the twins. He picks his daughter up on time every two weeks, like him and Sara agreed from the beginning. April, Solomon and Sara's child is so sweet and respectful with a lot of manners and home training. Eve and day love their half-sister, but it never fails; they always end up jumping her when it's time for her to go back home to Sara. Christina adores April. They seem to have a great relationship with each other, better than her own two. Christina accepted April and respected Solomon for being truthful about the whole situation. Back when Christina would visit Solomon at Camp 15, Sara would give her hard stares. After Solomon ran down his story to her about them bumping uglies on a regular basis while locked up; Christina understood why she had the attitude and tried to murder his ass in the hospital that night.

Solomon's career as a filmmaker and actor is steady on the rise. After his documentary aired on 48 hours, his status as a film maker documentarian placed him amongst the elite in Hollywood. He's made several appearances in motion pictures and is now a permanent actor on a weekly series called L.A.P.D. Blues.

There's been a lot of tension amongst the Blacks, Koreans and police throughout Los Angeles County. Blacks complain about Koreans being rude to them while purchasing their items at the local stores and swap meets, in their hoods. Koreans follow Blacks through the aisles of liquor stores and supermarkets, making them uncomfortable when shopping. If you're black and driving, you're getting pulled over by the cops no matter if you had all of your credentials or not. This grew a thick cloud of tension over the greater Los Angeles County. A black motorist high on P.C.P was beaten senseless by the police and is now on trial for their unjust actions. Also, there has been talk about a gang truce amongst the

Bloods and Crips, in an effort to stop the black on black crime and killings amongst black men.

Solomon is alone with his two kids babysitting while Christina is out taking care of business. He sits in the den watching rap videos on the Box. This is a channel that show videos upon request of the buyer for 99 cents apiece.

Eve and Day are bouncing off the walls and furniture, hyper off something that they ate containing sugar earlier.

"FUCK YOU! FUUUCK YOOUU! Day yelled, from the top of his lungs, flipping Solomon the bird with both hands. For the umpteenth time Solomon has pleaded with these two demons to please stop cursing at him. They're not trying to hear it though.

"Daddy, turn it to MC Hammer!" Eve screamed, lying on her back next to him on the floor.

"Okay, wait until this video goes off," Solomon

responded in a calm manner, face glued to the screen.

Eve quickly jumps onto her feet with her fist balled up frowning. "I SAID NOW!"

"No baby you have to wait," Solomon explained, hoping that she doesn't take it there. She runs off only to return with a Duracell C battery in her right hand. She stops several feet behind Solomon hurling the battery at him, but missed. The battery struck the side of the T.V., Eve turned around and got in the wind laughing.

Solomon ordered two videos by MC Hammer, Turn this mutha out and U can't touch this. Solomon turns it up loud. As soon as they hear it, they dash into the living room and stand right in front of the television, dancing.

Solomon cellphone rings. He answers it on the third ring, but the person on the other end doesn't say a word. He hangs up.

"Both of y'all get dress," Solomon ordered, to the

two little brats. They ignore him and continue doing the running man. "Hey, do y'all want a happy meal or not!?"

They heard that statement loud and clear. Without even replying to his question, they run past him to put their clothes on. In a matter of five minutes, they were both fully dressed. However, their hair is uncombed. He wasn't tripping, he'll find someone in the hood to comb it.

*****

Solomon pulled up to the front of China's residence in a burgundy 1992 Ford Explorer Eddie Bauer. Eve and Day are in the back seat scarfing down whatever is left of their happy meals. China walks through the front yard excited, dying to see her grandchildren. Solomon hardly comes through his old turf, now that he's a star. Every time he comes through, China would beg him to bring the kids so that they could get to know each other. Now they're all here, let's see how it unfolds.

China arrives to the back passenger window excited. Solomon rolls it down already knowing how it's about to go down.

"Hey, there go my grandbabies. Come give granny a hug," China begged, smiling at the two. They both heard her looking at her examining her face. Her mug didn't register on the familiar list, so they both just stared not responding to that grandma trick.

"Oh, these two came straight from hell. You got your work cut out for you," Solomon explained laughing, as he exited the vehicle.

"Get back in here! Don't leave us by ourselves!" Eve shouted, from the top of her lungs.

"Shut yo' ass up!" Solomon responded, as he walked around the truck, going through the yard and in the house.

"Oh my God," China replied shocked, of how

Solomon interacts with her grandbabies.

"Who are you?" Day asked sarcastically, looking China straight in the eye.

"I'm your grandmother. I'm Solomon's mother," China explained, hoping that'll get them moving. Wrong.

"So what," eve shot back, getting China in her feelings. She opens the back passenger's side door to let them out.

Day flings the toy from the happy meal at China, hitting her right in the mouth. The twins crack up laughing. China grabs her lip, her feelings are crushed that her grandkids are reacting to and treating her this way. Karma's a bitch, this is how she carried Solomon when he was young.

"Are you going to comb our hair?" Eve asked, as she met China at the door.

"Yeah, granny is going to comb both of you guys hair," China smiled, hoping that they were through with the bullshit, as she extended her arms out to them. "Come on, come with granny."

"Come on Day, she gonna do our hair. Come on Day Day!" Eve pleaded, looking at her brother who was frowning at China.

"Move!" Day shouted, pushing her arms out the way. China backed up several feet away from the truck. Day came to the edge of the trucks back seat looking in both directions, then jumped onto the pavement and dashed into her residence. China closed the trucks door and walked through the yard holding Eve's hand, until they reached the inside of her residence.

Solomon was chilling on the couch organizing his wallet, getting everything in order.

Day climbed on top of China's coffee table and started jumping up and down, demanding music.

"Get off the coffee table baby, okay?" China asked respectfully, trying to be friends with her grand babies.

Day just gave her a strange look not moving a muscle. China has had enough of their bullshit, now she's gonna have to start pushing a line. "Get your ass off of my coffee table!"

With both hands like a professional. Day calmly flipped China the bird frowning, letting her know that she doesn't run shit but her mouth. "FUCK OFF!"

China can't believe the nerve of these little bastards getting at her like this. "I'm whooping your little bad ass."

"Oh, no you not!" Day shot back serious. "I wish you would!"

Deena and Sabrina strolls through the front yard coming over to see their famous brother, after noticing his truck out front. They walk inside.

"Big bro, how you doing?" they both asked, excited to see Solomon.

"Oh, I'm good. Just sitting here fixing my wallet

and watching your mother deal with her grandkids," Solomon responded smirking.

They both look at Day who is standing on top of the coffee table still refusing to get down, on one.

"Can you braid my hair like my daddy's?" Day asked, talking to Deena and Sabrina. He jumps off the table growling when his feet touches the floor.

"Ooh, I'm scared of you." Deena replied laughing.

"You better be," Day shot back, walking up on his auntie with both fist bald-up frowning.

Sabrina cracks up laughing hitting her right leg with her right hand. "We got our work cut out for us."

China gives Deena a comb and a jar of Blue Magic hair grease. Deena snatches Day up and sits down with him in the recliner, putting him in between her legs. China places Eve in a chair from the kitchen and does her hair. The telephone rings that is sitting next to Solomon on a wooden stand.

Solomon looks up at China to get approval to answer her telephone.

"Solomon see who's calling." China instructed, parting Eve's hair down the middle.

"Hello," Solomon answered.

"Um…may I speak to Linda please," asked the anonymous voice on the other end.

"May I ask who's calling?"

"This is Robert'"

"Okay, hold on. Roberts on the phone," said Solomon.

Chinas heart began beating overtime. This is Solomon's father. She drops what she is doing and runs to Solomon, grabbing the phone and running into her room closing the door behind her.

"What the fuck is she doing?" Eve asked, pissed that her hair is not done.

"We need to wash your mouth out with soap little girl," Sabrina stated, not knowing who she is dealing with.

"Bitch, I wish you would put some soap in my mouth. I'll call C.P.S. on your ass," Eve replied with conviction, looking her auntie Sabrina in the eyes.

The look sent chills down Sabrina's spine. She looked at Solomon to do something, he looked out the living rooms window. "Hmmph, these kids are some smart little demons."

"You better fucking believe it. Who's gonna stop us? We're untouchable," Day interrupted, getting his sisters back. "If you want us to behave you need to have some money, music or McDonalds. Period."

Deena and Sabrina looked at Solomon for some answers.

"You heard what they said and they're dead serious. Try them if you want to," Solomon explained, flashing a warm smile.

"Granny! You need to hurry up shit! Eve shouted, as she stood onto her feet, walking over to their grandmother's refrigerator opening it. After studying the inside of it, she becomes more upset that there is nothing inside for her and Day. She slams the door with all her might furious. "You think I'm playing?"

"Come on Eve, let auntie finish your hair," Deena pleaded, waving her hand at her to come in her direction. Day gets out of his aunties lap with three neatly twisted cornrows going to the back, with red rubber bands at the tip of them. Day climbs back on top of the coffee table grabbing his crotch singing *Fuck the police,* by NWA. Eve sits in between her auntie legs to get her hair done.

Sabrina looks at the children in disbelief. "I don't know what were gonna do with these two little angels."

Day points his finger at his auntie becoming serious. "Not a muthafucking thing. Our own parents can't stop us.   We only obey MC Hammer, Ronald McDonald and the eye of Horus."

"The eye of Horus, who is that?" asked a foolish Sabrina.

Eve interrupts their conversation laughing at her auntie. "You're so damn dumb. The eye that's on top of the pyramid, on the back of the one dollar bill."

Sabrina is stunned at the intelligence of her nephew and niece. She comes out of her front pocket with a one dollar bill examining it. "Oh wow, I never really tripped off that."

"Yeah, because you're part of the eighty five percent," Eve replied, confusing the hell out of her auntie.

Sabrina scratches her head out of confusion. She giggles out of embarrassment. "I'm scared to ask them about the eighty five percent."

"We already know, because you're hella stupid,"

Eve responded calmly, looking her auntie in the eye not blinking. "I can't stand your ass."

"I still love you niece. Ten years from now we're gonna look back at this and laugh," Sabrina expressed blushing at her niece. Eve continues to grill her auntie not saying a word. Sabrina is in shock.

Deena finishes the last ponytail on her nieces head. Then playfully grabs her face, kissing her. Eve gets upset wiping her face several times with both hands, in a way that only a kid knows how. "Thank you for doing me and my brother's hair. But don't you ever grab my face like that again with your gay ass."

China comes back into the living room with a different attitude, handing Solomon the phone to place back on the receiver.

"Put this over there Solomon."

Eve climbs onto the coffee table joining her brother in whatever. Day has a beef with his granny, he wants to see if he can make her cry. Eve is going to lay in the cut and play both sides. They both give China cold stares.

Solomon's pager goes off, without looking at it he stands up to stretch. "I need to make a run right quick. Y'all stay here with granny and your auntie's okay. I'll bring back some more Mc Donalds."

"Yes sir!" Eve shouted, from the top of her lungs, stomping her feet on the glass table. "I wanna stay because I love granny, daddy."

"Aww," the twins responded in unison.

"Okay, I'll be back and be good. Don't be showing out or I won't bring shit back," Solomon stated seriously. But it was a throw off, he already knows that once he's in the truck, they're gonna act of fool.

"Okay Daddy, we'll be good. We love you, BYE!" Eve playfully shouted.

"Alright, I'll be back," Solomon responded leaving

their residence, getting in the truck and bouncing.

Eve and Day remain on top of the coffee table looking at their siblings in silence. Deena sits in the recliner, while Sabrina fumbles with the TV to play some music videos. China stands in the kitchen by the window smoking a Newport, smiling at her grandchildren.

"We're getting bored, we need something to do," Eve stated calmly, looking around at her relatives. "Can you make us a cake granny?"

Sabrina finds a video channel that's playing 357's, *Yeah, Yeah, Yeah*, the two go bonkers dancing on the table. Deena and Sabrina crack up laughing. They love their niece and nephew, they remind them of themselves when they were this young.

Tina-Ru knocks on the door, interrupting the dance party the twins were having. Sabrina turns down the television. "Come in blood!!"

"What's happening blood? What y'all doing?"

Tina-Ru asked, to no one in particular.

"Babysitting these bad ass kids," Sabrina responded chuckling.

"You better watch your mouth," Eve responded, with her hands on her hips, rolling her eyes and neck. She looks at Tina-Ru and frowns. "Who is you? I hope you're not another one of our aunties, with your ugly self."

"Oooh, no you didn't," Tina-Ru responded laughing at them. "I see someone needs a spanking."

Eve and Day giggle at Tina-Ru's foolish remark.

"You got us fucked up," Day stated, looking at Tina-Ru walking up on her.

"Look! You guys are being very disrespectful. Y'all not gonna come over here and talk to grown-ups like that. You guys are kids!" China demanded getting loud, walking up on them pointing her finger.

"Hmph, ain't that a bitch. We're kids, we

supposed to be disrespectful, deal with it. We're gonna do what the fuck we wanna do and when we feel like doing it. You think I'm playing, huh?" Eve asked her granny seriously. Everyone in the house becomes silent, with a look of confusion on their faces. Eve jumps from the coffee table onto the couch and grabs the house phone off the charger and holds it in her hand while she verbally beats them down. "I can make one call and shut this whole fucking piece of shit house down. Don't try us."

China forms tears in her eyes, as she pleads with her grandchildren, who has the house under siege. Tina-Ru, Sabrina and Deena looks on stunned, not saying a word. Deena gets up and consoles her mom.

"We came into this world to personally give you a hard fucking time. Why? Because you gave our father a hard time when he was a kid. We're gonna dog your ass out until we feel like you had enough. Now the shoe is on the other foot and you don't like it huh?" Day becomes more furious with his granny. "Answer me!"

Tears stream down China's face on both sides. "Baby I'm your granny, that's no way to talk to me. I love both of y'all."

Eve hurls the phone at China, missing her face by inches. "Call my father and tell him that we are ready to get ghost. We're not never coming back either."

"Come on Eve, let's wait in the front yard before I go nuts up in this weak ass house," Day demanded, jumping off the table and walking towards the bar door. Eve follows behind. Day stands on his tippy toes to open the door, they both walk into the front yard and sit on the grass frowning.

China dries her face, embarrassed at how they just got at her. "I don't know what I'mma do with them two."

They all crack up laughing at the nerve of them demons.

"Well, on a different note, y'all know it's a gang of homies up at Magic Johnson Park having a meeting," Tina-Ru explained, taking a seat in the recliner seat by the door.

"What they meeting about?" Deena asked, out of curiosity, sitting on the sofa next to Tina-Ru.

"Well, it's been talk about a cease fire. The Bloods and Crips are gonna have a peace treaty and put the guns down. No more beefing," Tina-Ru responded.

"It ain't gonna happen, it's too much bad blood between us and them. I'm not fucking with no Bompton Rickets, (Crips) straight up," China explained, firing up another Newport as she looks through the bar door, checking on her grandkids. "Sabrina, go out there with the kids and keep an eye on them." Sabrina does so.

"Well, would you peace treaty with some L.A. Crips?" Tina asked, trying to see where her head is at.

China thought for a moment. "Yeah, I ain't got no

personal beef with them. I guess I could."

"Oh, today is the day that they supposed to read the verdict, of those police officers," Deena explained turning it to the news. Every news channel is talking about the verdict. They're gonna read the verdict at 4:00 pm. Deena glances at her wrist watch it reads, 3:45 p.m. "We got fifteen minutes."

The city of Los Angeles is at a breaking point. Groups upon groups of blacks are on stand-by, waiting for the final decision. If it's not the one they are waiting to hear, blacks vow to burn Los Angeles to the ground.

Fifteen minutes has gone by, everyone is standing around the television in China's residence, waiting on the verdict. News reporters from various stations are in front of the court building. The verdict is out: NOT GUILTY.

"Aw, that's fucked up! Ain't no muthafucking justice for a black man," Tina-Ru vented, folding her arms on top of her chest pissed.

China begins to tear up, she just couldn't believe how the justice system just slapped every African American in the face like that. "That's foul blood. That's hella foul!"

Sabrina puts her face up against the bar door. "Blood, its muthafuckas running down Avalon with a gang of clothes in their hands, like they just robbed the swap meet."

Deena turns to the local news, KTLA channel 5. As the anchor man talks about the verdict, fires are being set and people are running down the street looting and rioting, on live television. "Aw man it's on. I'm about to bell to the swap meet."

"Blood lets bell down there," Tina responded, jumping out of the recliner onto her feet.

Solomon pulls up in front of China's residence with his hazard lights on. He nervously jumps out and runs to the fence to grab Eve and Day. "Come on y'all, it's time to go."

"Bye Sabrina, fuck everybody else," Day expressed, as he and his sister exited through the gate and got into the truck.

"Man, I have to take my kids home to their mother. Everybody is burning shit up and looting. I just passed the Avalon swap meet and they're tearing that muthafucka up. It's on and popping," Solomon stated, with a wide grin on his face; But at the same time is not trying to stay.

China, Deena and Tina-Ru join Sabrina out in the front yard.

"What's popping?" asked China, eager to get into something.

"Solomon said he just passed the swap meet, niggas in there taking shit from the Koreans and burning shit up." Sabrina explained, getting pumped ready to participate in some looting.

"Hey, I gotta take my kids home," Solomon stated,

jumping back in the truck and mashing out.

"Bye grand babies," China shouted, waving at the truck as it sped off.

"Let's bee (see) what's popping at the Avalon," Deena stated, leading the pack out of the front gate.

*****

Everybody and their mama is running in and out of the swap meet with stolen items. Cars are driving recklessly up and down Avalon Blvd blasting rap music. Building after building is set ablaze. Fire fighters try their best to put out fires, but in certain areas they don't even respond, due to being shot at. Koreans try to outsmart pilfers by spray painting black owned on the windows of their place of business. The only thing that did was piss blacks off, for playing them like they were stupid. Police just stood back and watched as the city went out of control.

China, Deena, Tina-Ru and Sabrina finally made it

to the swap meet. The inside was in shambles. Everyone just grabbed whatever they could and got on. Whatever they got was a come up, it was free.

China got lucky and found a shopping cart, as she exited the building, dashing through the parking lot.

She tossed her items inside and pushed the shopping cart down Avalon, in the direction of Vons supermarket.

"Blood, hold up!" yelled Deena, with an armful of clothing. She catches up with her mother and tosses her items inside the cart. "Are you going to Vons?"

"Yeah, I need some food, to hell with that other bullshit," China expressed, pushing the shopping cart with force. Around five minutes later, they arrive at the supermarket. People are running in various directions, grabbing anything that is worth stealing. China and Deena arrives at the produce and meat section and take whatever is left and heads back to the house.

*****

In a matter of three hours, Los Angeles was burnt down to the ground. Foolish rioters didn't realize that they destroyed their own neighborhoods. There wasn't any law enforcement in sight. All the agencies from the inner city was called to the suburbs, to help the police in that area keep the looters at bay. The once talked about peace treaty is now if full effect. Bloods and Crips were rioting and looting, side by side getting money, there was no time to set trip. The Jordan Down, Nickerson Gardens, and Imperial Courts, were a safe haven for any gang member to hangout, no matter where you were from. Bloods were dating and partying with Crip women and vice versa. Crash units couldn't stand the sight of red and blue bandanas tied together. They had to figure out a way to break this up, because they knew at any given time, they could be a victim. The heat is on.

FIVE

May 12, 1992   Saturday 12:35 p.m.

OFFICER Milano is a part of the crash unit, (Community resource against street hoodlums) a unit put together within the L.A.P.D., who specifically target gang members. However, this unit only targets black and Hispanic men, allowing officers to violate their rights at will. Chief Daryl Gates, has a zero-tolerance policy, when it comes to gang members. If a gang is up under an injunction, members from that neighborhood cannot hang in a group of three. If so, you can be placed in jail.

Authorities have to figure out a way to put this truce to an end. Bloods and Crips constantly disrespect officers by letting their weapons hang from their pockets, daring them to be bold enough to try and make an arrest, while they're out-numbered.

Milano has been laying low since Christina has left him. He's been meeting up with Tina-Ru occasionally getting an update of Solomon and his ex-wife's activities. The news of her having twins, deepens his quest to chop Solomon's head off. He and officer Truman cruises down Avalon Boulevard, behind a money green 79 Coupe de Ville lowrider, on 14x7 hundred spoke Dayton wire rims. The vehicle is full, carrying five occupants dressed in red and blue clothing. Milano trails them for several blocks, then blurps (siren) them. The Cadillac keeps mashing, not paying the pigs any attention.

"Green Cadillac Pull over!" officer Milano ordered, getting upset with the occupants inside for showing him and his partner a lack of respect. Milano blurps the siren one more time, demanding that they pull over. "Green Cadillac. I said pull over now!"

The car pulls over on a hundred and nineteenth and Avalon, then the car drops flat onto the ground hugging the concrete. Milano and Truman is itching to kill some young disobedient gang members, who show no regards to the law. They both creep up on the side of each door with pistols drawn.

The driver of the Cadillac rolls down his window, unleashing clouds of chronic smoke into Milano's face. This is Turtle from 43 gangster Crip. "Was'sup cuzz?"

"Put your hands where I can see them...now!" Milano demanded, in a firm tone clutching his pistol, inches from Turtle's face. Turtle blows a kiss at officer Milano with a smirk on his face.

Officer Truman snatches open the passenger's door, so that the hoodlums can exit the vehicle from that side of the car. Five in total climb out of the car, two Bloods and three Crips; two which are females. Truman directs all of them to the hood of the Cadillac, to be frisked and interrogated. Truman goes inside of the vehicle tearing shit up looking for weapons and any other contraband items. Milano puts his gun in its holster and interrogates. As he shakes down Turtle, he notices Tina-Ru on the hood of the car looking opposite of his direction, hoping he doesn't bust her out. At the same time, Milano is trying to figure out a way to remove Tina-Ru away from the peace brothers, so that he can frisk and fuck her in a hotel room.

"They're clean, there's nothing but weed," Truman stated, to Milano as he shakes Tina-Ru down. Tina-Ru becomes highly irritated with him touching on her, being that he is not a female officer.

"Um, excuse me, don't you suppose to call a female to search me?" Tina-Ru asked sarcastically, knowing her rights.

"Yeah, she's right Truman. Shake those Bloods down," Milano ordered, he wanted to time this move with precision. He stopped frisking Turtle and walked up to a nervous Tina-Ru. "What is your name?" I'm checking all you douche bags for warrants. "I don't like your stanking ass attitude."

Tina cleared her throat. "Tina Lucas."

Officer Milano walked over to the other female and interrogated. "What's your name?"

"Sherry Davis," replied Sha-Loc, from Four Deuce Gangster Crip.

"Alright, you guys hang tight while I run you guys for warrants," Milano stated, as he climbed into the driver's side of his vehicle, checking the names on his radio. Tina-Ru already knows what time it is, she continues to nervously look around at everything around her except for Milano. Truman is finished frisking the other scumbags for contraband. Tension rise, moments later Officer Milano steps out of the vehicle with a devilish smirk onto his face. "Ms. Lucas, you have an outstanding warrant for your arrest." I'm gonna take you to the station then sight you out."

Tina-Ru forms a lump in her throat. She didn't feel like dealing with Milano and his foolishness right now. But she complied. "Alright."

Officer Milano cuffed her up and placed her in the

backseat. "Okay, the rest of you guys beat it... pronto."

The rest of the members quickly jumped back into the Cadillac, hitting a few switches raising the car up and speeding off down Avalon Boulevard.

*****

It's night time somewhere around 8:40 p.m. Tina-Ru and Officer Milano is occupied in a low key motel in Cudahy, a city that's next to Paramount, where hardly anyone would notice the two. They've been here for over an hour, licking and lapping on each other like it's the thing to do. Tina is ready to end this information and freak fest with Milano, but can't figure out a way.

Officer Milano has been single since his wife left him for Solomon. Tina-ru is his only outlet to get his nuts out the sand. If it wasn't for her, he'll be yanking on his noodle or purchasing some pussy, like the real trick that he is.

Tina-Ru comes from out of the shower drying

herself off with a big brown towel, getting herself together. Milano is chilling in the queen size bed, flicking through various channels, looking for something to watch until he gets his second wind.

Tina-Ru fires up a cigarette, while applying baby oil to her body, taking puffs in between.

"So, what's the latest and greatest?" asked Milano, as he tossed the remote onto the bed.

"As far as what?" Tina-Ru asked, playing the Jedi mind trick on Milano. She didn't wanna give up too much information, knowing that it could be used against her. Tina-Ru has to play chess.

"Come on, don't start acting like you're game goofy. I'm speaking about the latest shit around your neighborhood. My ex and that fucker that she ran off with."

Tina-Ru takes two more puffs from the cigarette, before disposing it into the ashtray that's placed on the dresser drawer. She contemplated on his question before answering it. "I mean...shit, Solomon doesn't hang out anymore. I'm talking about at all. I saw him with his kids a minute ago. And those kids ain't nothing nice. They're twins and they move on their own agenda. They don't respect nothing or nobody but, MC Hammer, Ronald McDonald and the eye of Horus."

Fucking Monkeys! I bet they respect some fried chicken and cherry Kool-Aid! Milano thought, lacing his fingers on top of his chest in deep thought of the foul act of betrayal that Christina put him through. That is the only woman that ever loved him. They've been together ever since they were sophomores at Carson high school, back in the day. Tina-Ru saw him in deep contemplation, so she decided to act fast. She walked onto the bed and sat on his face, grinding her cunt hard on his nose. Milano gave in and rubbed his face into her bush, meeting her every gyrating thrust. The two went on to have animal style sex all through the night; forgetting what they really came there for. That's the power of the pussy.

SIX

May 13, 1992   Sunday 7:30 p.m.

Chinadoll mashes her 76 Chevy Impala, west on Manchester Boulevard. She's going to hang out with Solomon's father Robert, to get the sexual release that she needs to get her scruples back in order. Because since she's been home, all she's been doing is snapping at everyone because she is frustrated sexually.

China still has her beauty intact and decided to dress up a little wearing tight clothing, however still flamed up staying true to her allegiance to the Piru gang. She gets caught at the red light at Manchester and Crenshaw. She clutches her 9mm handgun for safety precautions. Even though it's a peace treaty, this is the most dangerous stoplight in Los Angeles County. This area is claimed by the Inglewood Familys. A well known Blood gang from Inglewood that murder Crips just because. She looks at the parking lot to the right of her and notices several vehicles posted around what used to be a Rally's hamburger franchise. A few Blood members from Crenshaw Mafia, Inglewood Family and the Weirdos Blood gang flashes signs at China. She honks the horn and throws a Blood sign out of the driver's side of the window, as she pushes down Manchester Blvd.

China hasn't been out of her area in a minute. She looks in disbelief as she passes one burned building after another. She considers this part of town more upscale than where she lives. As far as she is concerned, these blacks over here was upper middle class. She looks at the new great western forum which is now royal blue. That's how long she hasn't been to Inglewood, because last time she passed by the forum it was red. She shook her head in disbelief chuckling.

Ten minutes and two cigarettes later, China pulls into the parking lot at the Holiday Inn and sits in her car for a moment, getting herself together physically and mentally before she goes inside. Ten more minutes goes by, China heads to the room.

*****

Christina and Solomon are cuddled up in their bed watching National Lampoon's 'Animal House.' Both of them are fans of old school comedy movies from the 80's. Eve and Day are knocked out sleep in their bedroom. So the two are going to cherish this moment, because they both know when the two wake up, they're going to raise hell.

"I forgot to ask you honey. How did the kids act when they went to visit their grandmother?" asked Christina out of concern.

"They performed well, they did her just like she done me when I was trying to love her. Except they did it from a kid's point of view, they didn't hold back their tongue or bad words. They even made her cry and threw her own house phone at her." Solomon explained, doubling over in laughter.

"Oh honey, that wasn't nice. How come you didn't stop them?" asked a curious Christina, in disbelief of how come they weren't spanked for being unruly.

"Shit, when I was getting jumped and verbally whooped on, nobody helped me shit. I had to fight everybody. Well not the twins they were cool. But everyone else fuck em! Fuck em and feed em fish." I even let them get on the twins helmet (head). Then I left for a minute, only to return with them already in the front yard ready to go," Solomon expressed, getting upset from the thought all over again. "Oh believe me, they'll stop harassing her when they feel that she had enough."

"I don't know where they get that energy from. They came out of my womb pissed off," Christina explained, rubbing her chin in thought.

"I know. I thought about that several times. They most definitely got it from me and my side of the family. Because we have some mental issues running through our genes," Solomon shot back chuckling. "You know, I just thought about something. The last time that I was over at my mother's house, she got a phone call from a man named Robert. He sounded like a white man."

"Who is Robert honey?" Christina asked out of curiosity, as they both sat up in bed against the head board.

"I'm not sure. I wanna take a wild guess and say my father, because when I told her who it was, she grabbed the phone and went into her bedroom to conversate. I thought that was kind of strange," Solomon expressed, shaking his head in disagreement. "I mean, if that was my father, she's out of pocket for not telling me,"

"You don't know your father at all?"

Solomon shook his head. "At all, don't know nothing about him. Except that he paid my mother for sex. So he may be well off or rich."

Christina thought for a moment. "I have an uncle name Robert. A real cool guy, no kids, no wife, lives alone in Santa Monica, in this huge house with a couple of dogs. Me and my father used to always visit him to keep him company. That's my father's brother and they were tight. I seen my uncle six months ago at the supermarket in Venice. Once my father passed, we hardly seen each other, except for that time at the market," Christina explained staring into space, rubbing her chin." That's how I got into real estate, through him. He's a big time real estate investor. I'm talking about big."

Solomon sat in deep contemplation. "You know, the next time I see my mother, I'm going to ask her about my father and his whereabouts and see if I could get in contact with him."

"Yeah, do that honey. That'll be great if you guys could get acquainted. I would pursue that if I were you," Christina professed, putting a positive thought in

Solomon's head.

Solomon pondered on that thought. "I have to do some filming tomorrow morning around 9:30, you'll have to keep the kids with you. I cannot take them to the studio, we won't get any work done. We have to tape five more episodes before we start airing on television."

Christina's smile lit up the bedroom. "I'm so proud of you honey. We have accomplished so much since we've been together, more than me and Donovan when we were married," Christina uttered forming a frown onto her face thinking about her ex.

Solomon agreed. "I'm so glad that I met you. Who knows where I would be right now."

"Well honey, it was meant to be," said Christina, kissing Solomon on the lips before lying back down.

Solomon slid down onto his back, with his fingers laced on top of his chest, in deep thought, thinking about China and this mysterious man named Robert.

*****

China sashays around in the luxurious hotel suite in a red bikini G-string and matching bra. The older China gets, the sexier she is starting to feel. She lies on the queen size mattress, firing up another cigarette, waiting patiently for Robert to arrive. She turns on the television to the channel five news on KTLA and turns up the volume. Robert walks through the door.

"Linda, how are you doing honey?" asked Robert, as he walked into the suite kissing China on the forehead. "What's wrong?" you seem a little agitated."

"Nawh, I'm good, just reminiscing," China responded, as she put the cigarette out in the ashtray.

"When am I going to be able to meet my son?"

"He never come around anymore, now that he's a T.V. star and all," China lied hating.

"I mean does he have a phone number where I

can contact him?" Robert asked politely, not knowing why China is blocking his shot on meeting his son. He removes his shirt and pants and sits on the edge of the bed removing his shoes and socks, playing with his toes, sniffing his toe jam.

"The next time we hook up or better yet; the next time that you call, I'll have the number for you. I pinky swear," China lied again, she's starting to convert back to her old ways. Just being ignorant and not giving a fuck who she offends.

"That'll be nice. I have no clue as to what he looks like or nothing. Well, at least he's doing good from what you're telling me. He's not out their running the streets slanging rocks and shit," Robert responded, proud of what he heard about his son.

"No, he's not running the streets at all. He has two bad kids. You may not like those grand kids. They're super bad and they don't like or respect anybody but, Ronald McDonald, MC Hammer and the eye of Horus"

China explained, bursting out laughing at the thought of those crazy demands that they made that day.

"Robert laughed. "That's what they said?"

"Yep," China shot back smiling. "And they're only three years old."

"I would like to meet them one day also. I'm waiting on you," said Robert, sitting up on the bed board next to China getting comfortable. They watched the ten o' clock news, smoked a few cigarettes, then made love until the sun came up.

SEVEN

The Jungles is located on the west side of Los Angeles, in an area what is known as, The Baldwin Village. An upscale apartment vicinity, that is home to the Black P Stones. This area is a Blood haven to Bloods throughout the Los Angeles County. Jim Gillan Park is located in the center of the Jungles and is crowded with Bloods and Crips mostly off the west side of Los Angeles. Inside the gym, a basketball game is being played by the East siders versus the West siders, a combination of Bloods and Crips off the west side on one team and Bloods and Crips off the east side on the other.

Everyone is having a good time. Bloods and Crips from the surrounding areas and rivals to the P Stones are finally settling their indifferences. Crips no longer have to sneak in and out, to date females from here. It's all about love. Police from the southwest division cruise alongside the park, trying to figure out a way to break this festival up. Gang members flip officers the bird, as they make eye contact with each other. Everyone feels like the L.A.P.D. is just another gang in L.A. with guns and badges and has the authority to fuck over anyone at any time.

Solomon finds a parking space in the alleyway behind Jim Gillian Park. He jumps out of his convertible Corvette, dressed in red from head to toe, strolling towards the gym. The air is filled with chronic and cigarette smoke. Music blares from the D.J. booth that's set up in the center of the park, playing old school funk and rap music. Several people recognizes Solomon's face and acknowledges him, he appreciates the love returning nods.

He steps inside the gym looking around in awe, two large dice games are in full swing on opposite sides of the gym's court. The bleachers are filled to its maximum occupancy with Crips and Bloods, sitting in several different groups enjoying each other's company. The clocks buzzer went off when the player shot the final shot, from half court. The ball hit all net, Bloods and Crips ran around inside the gym going bonkers. The eastside team won.

"Solo! Solo! blood!" yelled Nine, from his wheel chair on the other side of the gym. Solo looks around and throughout the sea of faces trying to recognize the voice. From a distance, he sees Nine waving a burgundy bandana. He bells in his direction.

"What's popping blood? What you doing way out here in the wild wild west?" Solomon asked, reaching over giving Nine a hug, then some dap. They stroll out of the gym's back door, so that they can holler at each other in private.

"Blood, it's good to be (see) you love one. Last time I beed (seen) you, you were on 48 hours," Nine explained, chuckling, adjusting both of his legs in his wheel chair. "The young homie is coming up, I'm feeling that. It's your time blood, shine!"

"Oh, I'mma be on T.V. every week in a minute. I have a few more episodes to shoot then it's all to the good. I'm co-starring on this show called L.A.P.D. Blues. But the fucked up thing is that, I play a cop," Solomon added, seeing how Nine was going to respond to his new T.V. role as an officer. Solomon palms became clammy out of nervousness.

"What? That's good nigga. You're getting paid to be an actor homie, act. Fuck what people think, it's what we know. That shows your versatility, everybody can't do that, let along even have the opportunity to do so. God is good, stay positive and do your best and the roles will get bigger and better. Study your craft homie," said Nine, giving Solomon some positive motivation and encouragement.

Solomon nodded his head in agreement of what Nine expressed to him. That is why he and Solomon are so close. He wants to see his homeboy rise to the top, with no hating involved. That's rare, when you're surround by scumbags of a different feather. "I appreciate that homeboy real talk. You always know what to say."

"But always know young homie, it's from the heart," Nine expressed, flashing Piru gang signs with both hands. They do the handshake interlocking p's. "Well, on a more berious (serious) note. What brings you out this way young soldier?"

"I live on the other side of La Brea on San Tomas Drive," said Solomon, adjusting his Pittsburgh Pirates baseball cap onto his head.

"Oh, that's right over there. Baldwin Hills is nice. I'm thinking about moving back down to L.A.," said Nine, giving what he said some thought. "Nawh, I ain't fucking with L.A. County. I'mma stay in Apple Valley. Just like the saying goes, if it ain't broke then don't try to fix it."

Three females barged from the gym's back door giggling. This is Coco, Ty-Stick, and Henny, members of the Rolling Ninety's Crip gang in south Los Angeles. They slid back there on purpose trying to get an up close and personal look at Solomon.

"What's up with y'all gangsters? Where y'all from?" asked Ty-Stick, a five foot seven, one hundred and thirty pound, caramel complexion beauty, with curves that a man would die for.

"We both from Rolling One thirty Piru, where y'all from?" asked Nine, sizing all three females up from head to toe.

"Ninety Crip, "Ty-Stick responded, flashing a Kool-Aid smile. She looks over at Solomon feigning. "Where do I know you from?"

Solomon shook his head in deep thought, trying to put a name with the face. "I don't know, I don't think I know any Crips from Nine-0."

"Now you know me. I'm Ty-Stick, Ty or Lady Ty-Stick, whichever name that you can remember," Ty stated, extending her hand out to Solomon shaking his. She then shakes Nine hand. "Oh, these are my other home girls from the hood. This is Coco and Hennessey." They all shake hands.

"Hey y'all, I'mma go back in the gym and see what's cracking up in there," said Co Co, she sees that she's the fifth wheel and doesn't want to fuck off their couple action, so she decided to bounce.

"Aright, you know where we are at if you need us," said Hennessey, taking a seat on Nine's lap getting acquainted. Nine puts his mack down.

"You're kind of sexy. How many girlfriends do you have?" asked Ty-stick, pushing up on Solomon aggressively. She couldn't help it, she wants to jump Solomon's bones.

Solomon flashes a smile. "I don't have any girlfriends I have a soon to be wife and three kids and two baby mamas."

"Well, I ain't gonna beat around the bush. I'm trying to fuck with you. I know you love your wife or whatever, I ain't tripping. I'm trying to get married. I'll be the side bitch. I'm just trying to get in your business, sexy Blood," Ty-Stick confessed, not holding back her feelings.

"Oh yeah, we most definitely can fuck with it," Solomon replied, hugging on Ty-stick, palming her ass cheek with his right hand. Ty is loving every minute of Solomon's company. "Are you busy right now?"

"No, why? Was-sup?" asked Ty-Stick blushing, already knowing what's on his mind. She ain't tripping though.

"Come and take a ride with me," Solomon replied, in a more serious tone.

"I ain't tripping let's go," said Ty-stick, rising to the occasion.

"Don't take my home girl somewhere and kill

her," stated Hennessey joking.

I'mma kill this pussy. Solomon thought to himself. "Kill her? Why would I do that?"

"I'm just clowning. You got too much going for yourself. I know you wouldn't do nothing that stupid," Hennessey expressed blushing.

"Nine, I'mma holla at you later big homie," stated Solomon, as he strolled off with Ty-stick with his arm around her neck.

"Alright young homie," nine responded.

*****

Milano and Truman sits in the parking lot at Enterprise Park with their lights out, carrying on in conversation, plotting. Milano glances at his Seiko watch, which reads 9:03 p.m.

"I wonder how long is this damn peace treaty going to last?" asked Milano, adjusting his gun that's on the side of his holster.

"From the looks of it, no time soon," Truman

replied, shaking his head thinking about it. "These ignorant son-of-a-bitches burnt down their own hoods. Tax payers are going to have to pay up the ying-yang trying to rebuild this shit hole."

"Yeah, they did a good job of it too. The air is still filled with a charred wood smell," Milano replied, looking throughout Enterprise Park which is a ghost town.

Before Milano and Truman could utter another word, their back window had collapsed from a bullet. The two officers nervously snatch their pistols from their holsters, horrified. The next bullet knocked out the window behind Milano, causing him to panic even more. Whoever this anonymous sniper was, took their time strategically firing rounds at the two cops. Milano calls for back up.

"Officer needs assistance! Officer down we need assistance at Enterprise Park!" yelled Milano, through the hand held radio. Within three minutes, police vehicles filled the parks parking lot with sheriff deputies, ready to kill anything moving. Several officers search alongside the brick wall that separates the park, from residents' homes.

Truman and Milano are outside of the vehicle
explaining to their chief, about where they think the
bullets came from. Whoever this sniper was slid in and
out, before the backup arrived and eluded the ghetto
bird. Patrol cars zoom up and down the neighborhood
blocks, only to come up empty handed. Milano is
beyond pissed, deep in the back of his mind someone is
going to pay, but who?

*****

"Ooh shit, slow down daddy," Deena pleaded, as
she gets those guts beat up. Deena found her a dude up
at Athens park yesterday, when the bloods and Crips
had a barbecue there. Her new lover is Jimbo from
Underground Crip, a jet black, five foot ten, twenty five
year old jacker; who is a hot head trigger man for his set.
He's been slicing and dicing on Deena's coochie for the
past hour. This is the tune-up she's been looking for and
needing to get her mind back on track.

*****

Ty-Stick glances at Solomon occasionally, in
disbelief that she is actually riding through L.A. in a red
rag vette, with the blood that she saw on t.v. not too

long ago. Solomon pushes south on La Brea Blvd, in route to this tuck spot that he has in Inglewood that no one knows about. Not even his wife Christina.

Solomon looks over at Ty-Stick with a smirk on his face. "So, what's going on with you Lady-Ty? Tell me a little something about you, besides you being a sexy female Crip from Nine-o."

"Well, I'm twenty two with no kids. I don't want any until I get married or get financially stable. I don't wanna raise a child alone, because their daddy is in prison or dead," she explained whole heartedly.

Solomon chuckled. "Well, you better not mix and mingle with too many black men from the greater Los Angeles County. Because the penitentiary and mortuary is almost promised...shit."

"How did you elude the two?" asked Ty-Stick, trying to drop a hint that she wants Solomon to pump one up in her.

Solomon pondered on her question before answering. "The woman that I live with now, helped me in more ways than I could imagine. She gave me that push that I needed and I'm grateful."

"God is good," said Ty-Stick.

"All the time," Solomon responded with the quickness.

They pull into the driveway of a residence located somewhere in Inglewood on Tamarack Avenue. They got out the car and went inside.

"Make yourself at home," Solomon stated, removing his baseball cap and jacket, tossing it onto the couch. Ty-stick undid her two braids that were in a rubber band down her back. "What are you mixed with, if you don't mind me asking?"

Ty-stick blushes. "No, I don't mind. I'm black, Native American and Mexican."

Solomon nodded in approval. "I'm black, Asian and white."

"Oooh, we'll have some pretty kids if we mix all those races together," Ty stated, dropping another hint on Solomon.

EIGHT

June 1, 1992   Tuesday 3:50 p.m.

Solomon left his daughter April, with China so that they could get acquainted with each other. April's behavior towards China is much different than Eve and Day's. China felt that her grand daughter was a peaceful angel, compared to those other two little bad muthafuckas. But she understood that they were kids and she loved them all, not taking their last visit personal.

Solomon pulls up and parks his Eddie Bauer in front of Chinas residence. He bangs on the bar door which is locked.

"Hold on a minute, shit!" China yelled, as she walked from her bedroom to the bar door, to unlock it for Solomon to let him in.

Solomon walks in and sits on the couch. "How did April act?"

"Oh, she's such a sweetheart. She's heaven sent. I adore her," China professed firing up a cigarette.

As on cue, April walks from the bedroom into the

living room. She sees her daddy and becomes excited. "Daddy!" she runs over to Solomon and jumps into his lap giving him a hug. Solomon hugs his daughter back.

China walks off for a minute, returning with a number scribbled down on a piece of paper. She looks over the piece of paper, making sure that it's correct, before handing it to Solomon. "Here Solomon."

He accepts the paper from his mother and stares at the unfamiliar number, trying to figure out; who, what, when, where and how. "What's this?"

China exhales taking her last puff off the cigarette, before tossing it out into the grass. "That's your father's number, he wants to hear from you."

Solomon was taken aback of what he just heard. He just stared at the number without saying anything. Inside, he was elated but confused. China looked on with tears forming into the wells of her eyes. The room was filled with an awkward silence for over three minutes before anyone spoke. Solomon cleared his throat. "Was that him that called the last time that I was here?"

Without uttering a word China just nodded her head in agreement. Solomon was speechless and felt betrayed all at the same time.

April playfully stuck her finger into her father's mouth. "What's wrong daddy, are you okay?"

"Yeah daddy's okay baby, just thinking that's all," Solomon replied, folding the paper up and placing it in his pocket. He really wants to chew China out for hating. But he had a better plan, he's going to let Eve and Day spend a weekend with her. "Has he been trying to contact me?"

"Well...he found me when I was in the county jail, fighting that murder. We were together about a month ago and I told him all about your status and your children. He can't wait until you call, he's dying to meet you, China expressed, feeling much better now that she released the info that she's been holding back from her son. She blazes up another Newport out of nervousness.

Solomon shook his head in agreement, in deep thought. "Thank you. I appreciate it."

*****

"So, you mean to tell me, you don't know or heard anything about some Bloods shooting at the police up at

Enterprise Park not too long ago," asked an angry Milano, trying his best to grill information from Tina-Ru but it's not working. Milano paces back and forth in the rooms minimal space in deep thought.

Tina-Ru shrugs her shoulders. "I don't know anything about no shooting at Enterprise Park. Whoever did that, is not going to share that type of information. That could put someone away for life, that has to be a secret."

"How long is this damn peace treaty supposed to last?" Every-time I roll through, it's a big ol' party. Fried chicken, barbecue and marijuana," Milano expressed, sounding a little bit racist.

"Hey, I don't know. Your guess is just as good as mine," Tina replied, getting a little upset with Milano and his weak ass game he's playing.

"I feel like you're not telling me everything. You suppose to have information for me every-time we meet up…. But nooo, you don't be knowing shit," Milano responded, in a sarcastic way pissed off at Tina and her shenanigans. "I don't know what to tell you. All I can say is that, everything has been cool since the Bloods and Crips called a truce," said Tina Ru, keeping it real. But that's not the answer that he wants to hear. Milano's temperature is rising by the moment, he wants to personally kill the shooter and break up that fucking nigger festival called the peace treaty.

NINE

June 2, 1992   Wednesday, 5:00 p.m.

"I'mma burn this muthafucking house down to the ground!" yelled Day, with a large black bic lighter in his right hand. "I'm sick and tired of living in this shit hole! I wanna move to Africa, to the Amazon jungle!"

Solomon is at home with the kids while Christina is out handling business ventures. Solomon studies his father's phone number, but hasn't built up enough courage to make a call to him. He sits in front of the television on the couch, with his house phone on the side of him anticipating to make that move.

"I'm in the mood for some fucking Mc Donalds! I'm tired of eating this other bullshit!" Day yelled, pointing at the wall grilling whoever he sees on it.

Eve looks on cracking up at her brother who is over there tripping. "Day who are you talking to?"

"This fat muthafucka that's sitting on the wall.

109

Look, come here," Day replied dead serious. Eve walks over to where he's at and stares at the wall, trying to see what he is seeing. She squints her eyes adjusting her vision, still nothing, so she plays it off.

"Oh, now I see that muthafucker. It's Mickey Mouse, Pac-man and Barney the purple dinosaur. I think they're about to rob a bank... Look," Eve explained, walking up closer to the wall to get her man. She stops for a brief second, then walks up to the wall and spit, but the saliva lands onto her shirt. They both burst out into laughter. "Fuuuck you! Fuuuck yooouuu, you son-of-a-bitch! I'll burn all of you to fucking hell!"

"Shut up and sit ya'll punk asses down!" Solomon demanded, giving them a look of seriousness that read ass whooping.

They both slowly walked out of the living room, in route to their bedroom, so that they can make all the noise that they want. As soon as they got in the hall way, Day threw the lighter at Solomon as hard as he could,

missing his face by inches, hitting the lamp post.
Solomon looks down the hallway at them, they both flip
him the bird with both hands, sticking their tongues out,
dashing into their room laughing.

Solomon shakes his head at the two hooligans.
Now that he's alone and the noise level is at a minimum,
he's contemplating phoning his Dad. But what will he
say to him? He rubs his sweaty palms together, trying his
best to get them dry. He stares at the phone while
wiping his hands onto his pants leg. He pulls out the
number from his front pocket and studies it for a
moment. After thirty seconds of studying the digits, he
calls.

The phone rings twice. Solomon tooted his ass to
the side and let a silent but deadly one out, that reeked
of egg salad and root beer barrel candies. On the fourth
ring, Robert picks up the phone.

"Hello," said Robert.

"Um, hello, is this Robert? asked a nervous

Solomon.

"Yes, this is me. May I ask who's calling?" Robert asked, already knowing that it's his son, he's just making sure.

"Hey, this is your son Solomon. How you doing?" Solomon asked, breaking the ice, but at the same time exhaling from relief.

"Well, I'm doing a whole lot better now that I finally reached you. Your mother kept saying that she was going to give me the number, but never did," Robert explained, happy as hell that he is talking to his son.

The two conversated over the phone for two hours, with no interruptions. Day and Eve ran themselves tired and ended up falling asleep. It was perfect timing for Solomon, who closed their bedroom door and caught up on lost time with his pops. They exchanged numbers, then made a scheduled date to meet up with one another, when their busy schedules were unoccupied. Solomon was glad that he made that call. He feels like a building has been lifted off his

shoulders.

*****

The GRASS ROOTS football league was created

when the peace treaty started. Since its beginning, there

has been no violence whatsoever, everything has been

all good amongst the two color barriers. It's seven thirty

p.m. and both teams were in practice up at Enterprise

Park, for several hours. Like always, every get together

turns into a picnic or block party and this is what police

hated the most. Because they know that anytime that

you have all of these hooligans bunched up in one spot,

there's most definitely some handguns and assault rifles

in arms reach. The police must play chess. Out of

nowhere the ghetto bird (helicopter) zooms past the

park, only to bust a U-turn in the air and irritate the

gangbangers down below. Every gangbanger know how

hard it is to shake the bird once it gets on you.

Intoxicated members wave their bandanas at the bird,

followed by gang signs and middle fingers. The bird gets lower and lower as it circles around the park full of hooligans.

Patrol cars zoom toward the park with force, from every available direction putting pressure on the scoundrels. The element of surprise, caused pandemonium. Bloods and Crips ran to their vehicles trying to elude the officers, who blocked off the main entrance with their patrol cars. Other members avoided their vehicles altogether and took off running in the opposite direction tossing their weapons when they had the opportunity. Within a matter of ten minutes, officers had the area under siege. Back up officers came from other divisions, along with the National Guards, to put these villains in check. Whoever got away, got away. But seventy percent of the party goers and football players were spread out on the football field on their stomachs. Shit is getting ugly. Officers found numerous amount of handguns and pocket knives in the vicinity. Cops just collected them, but couldn't place them on anyone because they were not caught with them in their possession. Several patty wagons pulled up and were instantly filled, due to individuals having traffic and outstanding warrants. Majority of the women that had children with them, were allowed to leave without going through all the bullshit.

Milano walked through the crowd of drive by shooters with a chip on his shoulder. He wants some answers, as to who shot his patrol car up when him and Truman was carrying on in conversation that day. He sees no familiar faces and becomes even more upset. He looks over at the crowd of females who are sitting on the curb, getting questioned by female cops; in search of Tina-Ru. To no avail she's missing in action.

Officer Milano stands in the middle of the football field with a funky attitude, with both hands place on his hips like a super hero. Somebody's life is in danger, according to all the negative images and messages that's flashing across his dome. He needs to act out and fast. But what Milano doesn't realize is that, karma is a bitch and she doesn't discriminate as to who she repays her debt to.

TEN

June 8, 1992   Tuesday 2:35 p.m.

Solomon sits inside, the Salmon Grill a high end restaurant that's located on the west side of Los Angeles, in an area known as Santa Monica. He sits at the bar nervously drumming his feet against the foot stool, sipping on gin and tonic, waiting for Robert to walk through the door. He places an order of pot stickers sautéed in peanut sauce as an appetizer, as he awaits his father's arrival.

Ten minutes later, a white man dressed in a black Armani suit walks through the door. He's around five foot nine in height, and weighs about two-hundred pounds even. His salt and pepper hair and facial hair is well manicured. Robert looks about fifty five years of age easily, but is in physical shape.

"Solomon," said Robert, in a low tone as he noticed him at the bar smiling.

"Hey, what's up pops," Solomon replied excitedly, walking up to Robert giving him a long hug. They finally meet, both of them are excited. They both sit at the bar.

"My goodness, I finally met my son. Man, you look great. You turned out to be somebody. I heard that you have a career in Hollywood as a film maker and actor," Robert expressed, folding his arms across his chest examining Solomon proudly.

"Yeah, I just happened to be at the right place at the right time. My soon to be wife is the key person behind my success. If it wasn't for her, my career wouldn't exist. I'm blessed. God is good," Solomon responded, with a proud look on his face.

"Well, I'm into real estate. I'm an investor. I've been doing that pretty much all my life. You have an older sister out here in Venice California, married with two kids. Other than that, my life is pretty simple. I'm single with no other children," Robert expressed.

"I have three children. I would've brought them

with me but, they would've caused a lot of problems. Two live with me and the other one live with her mother in the valley, Solomon explained smiling.

Robert and Solomon ended up hanging out with each other for over two hours, eating appetizers and sipping on booze. They vowed to stay in touch with each other in the future. They exchanged numbers and bounced.

ELEVEN

July 10, 1992   Friday 7:30 p.m.

"Happy Birthday!" everyone yelled in unison, scaring the shit out of Solomon. He's been out all day running errands, and had no clue that his mother China and Christina came together to throw him a surprise party at his home. Everyone was in attendance, all his Piru homies and even Sara, his other baby mother. Solomon walks inside giving everyone hugs and handshakes as he makes his way to the den, which is decked out with food and drink at anyone's disposal. Christina pulls him over to the table, showing him the huge cake that's decorated in a red bandana, with twenty-two candles on it.

Solomon turns to the crowd of friends. "Thank you everybody, I appreciate you guys coming to my spot, thank-you."

China turns up the volume to the stereo. All she

plays is R&B and Rap music from the 80's. She grabs her sons hand and dances with him. The song, "Back and Forth," by Cameo is bumping through the speakers. Alcohol, marijuana and cigarettes are in heavy rotation.

Sabrina took all the children, which was only five; three of Solomon's kids and two of his homeboys, to the game room supervising them, as they ate cake and ice cream and played video games.

After Solomon danced with his moms for two songs, he personally thanked each individual for coming out. However, he did this to also see who is inside of his residence where he lays his head at. His eyes almost pops out of his head when he notices, baby mama number one, in the cut looking like something to eat, in an all black body dress. Solomon gives her a hug and a peck on the forehead, then post up with her.

"Well, well, well you didn't expect for me to be here, huh?" Sara asked, in a sassy tone crossing her legs in a seductive manner.

"No, you were the last person I was expecting to see here. But I'm glad that you came. How you been doing?"

"Oh, you know. Another one, like the other one. Same shit, ain't nothing changed since I seen you two weeks ago," Sara explained, taking a sip from the red plastic cup of booze, that she had on the table.

"You're looking good," said Solomon, becoming horny looking at her cleavage.

Sara formed a smile onto her face, as she peeped the bulge in his pants. "You're looking better."

Solomon stood up chuckling, he didn't want to get started with the sex talk. Because all it was going to do is, get him fired up and he's gonna want a shot of pussy. He kissed Sara on the forehead and walked off, adjusting his boner that was noticeable inside his pants. He'll holler at her when he picks up his daughter. He strolled throughout the inside of his home, not seeing anyone who he didn't like. He checked the backyard, which were mostly occupied by his Piru comrades.

Solomon continued walking through his property, ending up in his front yard, which was vacant of party goers. He took a seat alongside of the bushes that's out the way, in his front yard. While in the middle of collecting his thoughts, he sees a grey crown vic slowly passing by. Solomon becomes alert and keeps his eye on the vehicle. The crown vic goes two more houses down, turning into a driveway, heading back into his direction. Suddenly, the car comes to a complete stop right in front of his residence. Moments later, a female exits from the vehicle and walks through his front yard, ringing his door bell. China lets the female in, shutting the door behind her. The vehicle slowly drives away as if they were memorizing something. Solomon's heart pounds in overtime of what he just saw. *That's the same crown vic that shot me blood!*

Solomon went back into the house, the same way that he came out. He must investigate this anonymous bitch that exited that vehicle. He comes into the den where majority of the people are at, and post up.

"Solo blood, what's bracking (cracking) Homey?" asked Tina-Ru, dressed in red from head to toe.

Solomon just stares at Tina-Ru in disbelief, not feeling how she arrived to the shin-dig. He catches himself, he has to keep this secret on the under. "What's up with a Piru blood?"

She gives him a hug. "Shit, just came from the hood. Ain't nothing going on over there."

I bet it ain't bitch, when you're cruising by in a narc car. "I heard that, we just over here celebrating my twenty second year on this earth. We ain't making no noise."

"That's what's up. Happy Birthday blood." She responded, with a shit eating grin on her face. She walks over to the food buffet on the table and make her a plate.

"Thank-you blood. I appreciate it," he shot back, with a look of confusion. He strolls to the kitchen where Christina is at and gives her a kiss and hug, trying to get what he had saw off his mind. He grabs a bottle of water and hangs out in the backyard with the homies.

"Solo blood, what's good love one?" asked Nine, as he pulls up next to Solomon dressed in all red.

"Aww blood, you know another one like the other one," Solomon responded chuckling. "Whatever happen to you and ol' girl we met in the jungles that night?"

"Oh, you talking about Hennessey? Oh she cool, that's my little Crip bitch, she go," Nine explained, with a smile on his face. Nine looks over both shoulders, making sure none of his baby mamas are around. "What happened with you and Ty-Stick?"

"Aw blood," Solomon replied whistling, shaking his head at the good freak session they had in Inglewood that night. "She go hard blood, on the homies."

Nine claps his hands at the thought. "Blood, I know she do. She was filling up those Guess jeans that she had on that night. On Piru."

"I took them down immediately. I'm thinking about pumping one up in her. On everything," Solomon responded, trying to figure out how he can switch this conversation to Tina-Ru getting dropped off by that grey crown vic.

"Homie, where the kids at? I wanna meet them," asked Nine, not knowing how bad them little muthafucka's are.

"Are you sure? I don't think I have enough energy to deal with them demons," Solomon explained exhaling.

"Okay, I'll meet the lil homies next time," Nine responded, a little disappointed.

Solomon walks to the game rooms back door, looking for Sabrina. He tells her to bring the twins and

April out so that they can meet Uncle Nine.

Sabrina was more than happy, because them two alone was driving her up the wall. She walks all three of Solomon's kids over to him.

"Eve, Day and April, come over here and meet your uncle," Solomon ordered in a firm tone. All three stand in front of Nine's wheel chair not saying a word.

"Hi, Uncle Nine. How are you?" said April waving her hand at him breaking the ice.

Nine reaches in his pocket and pulls out a wad of cash, giving April a twenty dollar bill. She smiles. "Thank-you Uncle Nine, I love you," she stated giving Nine a hug, then dashed back into the house where Sabrina was, to finish playing video games.

Eve and Day stared at Nine, studying his face. They looked at each other thinking of a master plan.

"How much money are you going to give us? We're twins," Day stated, with his arm extended, like a slot machine.

"How much do you want?" Nine asked, not knowing that these two muthafuckers are sharp. They look at each other giving the signal.

"Fifty apiece. We need a bird (hundred) because we're twins and we're special. We're not like these other kids. We go hard in the paint," Day explained, not cracking a smile.

"A closed mouth don't get fed. Uncle Nine got you," Nine replied, giving both of them a crispy fifty dollar bill apiece.

The twins are shocked that their extortion scam worked. They look at each other in disbelief, this also put Uncle Nine in the top four of the people and things that they obey. They grab Nine by the leg hugging him tight, letting him know that it's all love whenever they bump heads. Solomon looked on shocked, he couldn't believe how they accepted Nine in the top four. But then again money talks, bullshit runs a marathon.

"We love you Uncle Nine!" Eve shouted, from the top of her lungs, before they made their way back to the game room where Sabrina was.

"Alright, I love y'all too. Y'all be cool," Nine shot back smiling. Reverse psychology is a muthafucka.

"Blood, I ain't never seen them be cool with someone like that. You got the Midas touch," Solomon explained chuckling, adjusting his Pittsburgh Pirates baseball cap.

"Yeah. Uncle Nine has a way with the little ones. I cherish kids homeboy, ain't nothing like em," Nine responded wholeheartedly, shoving his bankroll back into his pocket.

"Let me do my rounds homeboy. I gotta keep my eye on everything and everybody. I have two baby mamas in one spot. Ya dig?" asked Solomon, playfully he gives Nine some dap and strolls back into the house. Truth be told, he's still tripping off of what he saw, when Tina exited that grey crown vic. He needs some answers.

He goes into the kitchen where Christina is sorting out food for the guest. "Babe, come here, let me holler at you right quick."

Christina looks at Solomon concerned. She didn't like the tone of his voice, she quickly came to his aid. "What's wrong honey is everything okay?"

I'm not sure, check it out," Solomon ordered, walking into their bedroom, sitting on the dresser drawer. Christina comes into the room, closing the door behind her so that they could have some privacy.

"What's wrong honey?" Christina asked, taking a seat at the edge of the bed crossing her legs, resting her palms on top of her knees.

"Did you invite Tina to this party?" Solomon asked, folding his arms across his chest, preparing to interrogate his baby mama.

Christina thought for a moment. "Are you talking about Lucas? Your Piru friend?"

Solomon nodded his head. "Yeah, Tina-Ru, the one that used to be in the classroom with me."

"Well, I didn't invite her personally. I just told your mother, to make sure that all of your friends showed up. I didn't even see her, is she here?" asked a naive Christina.

"Yeah, she's here… But the disturbing part is, I saw your husband drop her off, in that same gray crown Victoria that shot me up, a few years ago," Solomon explained, removing his baseball cap, setting it on the dresser.

Christina covers her mouth with both hands catching her breath as her eyes widen out of fear. "Oh my God. Honey I didn't mean to invite her. Should I get my handgun out of the closet? I'll do anything to protect my family."

Solomon rubs his chin in deep thought, staring at the carpet. "No babe, don't do or say anything to her or anyone in this party concerning this matter. Just keep your eye on her. From seeing that move, I don't trust her anymore. I wonder what the fuck she is up to."

Christina stands up and gives Solomon a long hug. "Babe, I thought that I was doing the right thing by inviting your whole neighborhood. I had no clue that she had something going on with my ex or I wouldn't have invited her. I know that she likes you or whatever but, not to the extinct that our safety would be in jeopardy."

Solomon pulled back from Christina. "I know. I know baby don't trip. It's not your fault, you did nothing wrong. You were just looking out for me, making sure that I was happy. I know you didn't mean any harm. Just finish what you were doing, but keep your eyes open. And remember, don't mention what we talked about to anyone."

"Got you babe," said Christina, giving Solomon the thumbs up, as she walks back into the kitchen doing what she was doing.

Solomon began pacing the floors minimal space in

his bedroom, in deep thought. Tina-Ru has to go no exceptions, but how? He's contemplating letting Nine know about it, but at the same time, he doesn't think that's a good move. This is something that has to be done and be swept up under the rug, at the same time. He has to play chess. There ain't no way that he's going to fuck off his career, stooping to her level with the bullshit. But if he don't knock her block off soon, she could possibly fuck off everything.

The light of knowledge has turned on inside of Solomon's head. This move can make him or break him. But one thing is certain and two things are for sure, it's gonna be put down no matter what. Solomon walks back to the area where baby mama number one is at. He sees Sara and sits next to her, so that he can put something on her mind.

"I see you found your way back home you little stray dog," Sara said playfully, giving him a naughty look, while fondling one of her micro mini braids in between her fingers. "Happy twenty two years on this earth baby."

Solomon blushes. "Thank you, baby mama, number one. It's always a pleasure."

"I like when you say that," Sara responded seriously. She hates to be second at anything. As long as he keeps her at the top of the food chain, she will be his puppet. Solomon knows that, that's why he keeps the jumper cables on her back. The game is cold, but it's fair.

"I like saying it...Shit, it's the truth," he shot back. They both chuckle, enjoying each other's company. Out of nowhere, Tina-Ru strolls through, in route to the restroom to go and take a shit.

"Solo blood, what's up homie? I'm in a rush. I need to take a gangsta." (shit) Tina-Ru explained as she acknowledge the two, but kept pushing being that the shit log was at the tip of her ass opening.

Sara nodded in response, but gave Tina a cold

look, as if she was an enemigo. She looked at Solomon squinting. "Is that your homegirl?"

"Yeah why? You know her?" Solomon asked, not thinking nothing of it.

Sara curled up at the lip, while shifting in her seat mumbling underneath her breath. "That bitch ain't cool."

"What you mean?" Solomon asked, looking at his baby momma with a keen eye.

Sara stood up from her chair. "Let's go and sit inside your car and holler."

"Okay..." said Solomon, as he lead the way in route to his Eddie Bauer. They slid out the door by the game room through the backyard and inside the truck, that's in the driveway, clear of any party goers. Once inside, Sara stuck her tongue inside her baby daddy's mouth with force. They kiss each other long and passionate for a minute, then Solomon pulls back nervously. "Not right here baby momma, this ain't the time and place for making love."

"You're lucky, you little sexy mother fucker. I was going to sit on your face and smother you with this pussy," Sara stated in a vulgar tone, rubbing her legs like a cricket, getting aroused at the thought.

"I'm tripping off of what you said in the house," Solomon expressed, trying to put the pieces to this puzzle together, so that he can put this mess to the side and be the star that he's destined to be.

"Well, I was giving her fucked up looks because she ain't cool. You remember that day that you got shot, or night time, whatever? I was following that other gray crown vic because, I saw them on the same type of mission that I was on... That other crown vic is the police, I know that for a fact, and he works for the Carson Sheriff it's your second baby mama ex-husband. Apparently, that little black heifer caught a case and didn't wanna go to jail, so she started sucking, fucking and working for that son-of-a-bitch. Now, I don't know what she has up her sleeve exactly, but I know they're plotting on somebody. I done seen them hella times together. They favorite motel is in Cudahy, in a low key spot. I was already thinking about busting that bitches head wide open, just on the strength," Sara expressed, serious as cancer. She pulls out a cigarette from her purse and blazes it up, to calm her nerves.

Solomon was transfixed by what he had just heard from his baby momma. He knows that what she is saying is true, because as he thinks about it, it's all adding up. "I saw her get dropped off today, by that same gray crown vic... Her husband is seeking revenge on both of us. He wants her for leaving him and me for taking her. Now he knows where we live. Fuck!"

"Are you worried about them?" Sara asked nonchalantly, pulling on the cancer stick with one eye closed.

Solomon pondered on her question, hesitating to

answer. He shook his head.

"Don't be, continue doing what you do. You've come too far to drop the ball now. Fucking with these two cocksuckers, will take up too much mental space and that's something you don't need as an actor," Sara explained, keeping her baby daddy on track, because she really cares about him. "I'mma handle them, don't trip, you got my word on that. Just pick up your daughter every two weeks and fuck some sense into me, like you been doing and you're good."

Solomon reached over and gave his crazy, but down ass baby momma a long passionate kiss, for being who she is. "Thank-you baby momma number one. I don't know what I'll do without you... Thank you."

Sara blushed, knowing that her baby daddy appreciates her, made her feel good inside and out. "Just do me a favor and don't mention our conversation to nobody."

"Got you baby," Solomon responded, relieved.

Now he can get some sleep, because if his baby momma says that she got him, he's not going to question her get down. He knows that she's not working with a full deck. But he has the advantage, because she's on his team.

They both kicked it in the vehicle for another hour or so, conversating about their daughter. The rest of the night went on without any problems whatsoever. The party came to an end at a respectable time, everybody thanked Christina and Solomon, then went their separate ways.

TWELVE

January 3, 1993   Sunday 12:30 p.m.

Six months later

It's been eight months since foolish rioters burnt up their side of Los Angeles. But the city of Angels is slowly but surely, repairing itself for the better. Bloods and Crips are back at war with each other. However, the Watts area is still going strong and has no plans of breaking the truce. If a gang member wanted to still participate in cease fire, it is all love if you are in the Nickerson Gardens, Imperial Courts, or the Jordan Downs. The grass roots football league, is keeping the bandanas tied together on this side of town. And everyone is still welcomed.

Although many baby mamas and relationships were sprouted from this truce, some remained and some fell apart, being that most came from their worst enemies. One would have to be careful and play it by ear.

Police officers from every division were the most happy that gangbangers were back shooting at each other. They couldn't stand the sight of the two rivals at peace. Officers even went as far as to roll past picnics and other functions, shooting at them out of unmarked cars.

Solomon and his father has been seeing each other on the regular, even bringing the kids along to meet their grandfather. The twins bully him every time out of whatever, but he doesn't mind; he thinks it's pretty cool. Solomon's t.v. show, L.A.P.D. Blues is the number one show on television right now, making him a household name. It's hard for him to go out in public now, being that his face is recognizable. His stardom power goes both ways. When he's with kids, aggressive fans ask for autographs at the most inconvenient time, invading his privacy. On the other hand, store patrons close their stores off to the public, giving him shopping privacy. He knows that it comes with the lifestyle so he has to deal with it.

China and Robert still sees each other off and on, on a regular basis. Whenever these two are together, Robert rubs their relationship in China's face who had wished that she should've never gave him that number. China starting to hate again on the low.

Sabrina still live across the street from China, helping their grandmother out, whenever she's not working. She landed herself a job at the Cineplex movie theater, in Torrance California.

Deena also found a job at the Roadium swap meet on the weekends. On weekdays, she works at Foot Locker in the Del Amo Mall. She is also sprung on her Crip lover Jimbo, who she's been staying with off and on.

As for Tina-Ru, she's still slithering in and out of the neighborhood, meeting up with Milano, giving him the 411 on the latest and greatest. Most of the information that she gives him is bullshit, just a bunch of gossip to keep things at bay.

Sara has been watching Tina and Milano's every move, it's all about timing with her. Soon as she gets the opportunity they're both out of here, no exceptions.

Christina has a registered Glock 9mm handgun, that she has been carrying on a daily basis, since Solomon told her about that move, at the party that night. She'll be damned if she lets someone harm her and her loved ones. On the low, she's even been going to the gun range in Santa Monica, getting her shooting game back like it used to be. Christina, at one point used to be a handgun markswoman shooter, when she was with Milano. She's got her shot back, now it's on and popping.

*****

Ty-Stick is five months pregnant and happy, all at the same time. This was her plan from the jump, to get knocked up by Solomon. Solomon wasn't tripping, he just hopes that after the baby comes, she keeps her part of the deal. And that is, that she's now baby mama number three and she has to promise that she won't intervene with Christina and his family at home where he lives. Ty-Stick made a vow.

THIRTEEN

February 2, 1993   Friday 12:30 p.m.

China has been watching her grandkids since Wednesday trying to create some type of relationship. She wasn't feeling how they treated her on their last visit, so she decided to do it again, this time she has a weekend full of festivities planned for the three of them.

Eve and Day has only been over China's house for an hour and already they have been causing havoc on the Chinadoll. They're both on top of the kitchen glass table, armed with a wooden spoon and a rolling pin ready to kick something off.

"You feel hella dumb! You feel hella dumb! You feel hella dumb! You feel hella dumb!" they chanted in unison, stomping their feet and banging the spoon and rolling pin against the table, while they clown China. China looks on trying to figure out a strategy. She can't let her grandkids defeat her in her own house.

145

"Get y'all asses down, now! Y'all not gonna come over here and do what the fuck y'all want to do. Get down now or I'mma whoop y'all asses!" China ordered, with fire in her voice. She meant every word that she spoke, pointing her finger at the two. They become silent with a look of horror on their face. This time grandma means business. That shit she was talking didn't faze these two demons one bit. They both looked at each other and doubled over in laughter, pissing China off to the fullest.

"Mickey Mouse built a house, how many bricks did he need?" Eve asked China angrily.

"Fuck Mickey Mouse! I'm the big bad wolf!" China shot back, not realizing that she bit like a big mouth bass.

"No fuck you! Answer my question now or we will go into overtime on your ass!" Eve threatened, making China look and feel hella stupid.

China grabbed Eve off the table and swatted her

146

twice on the ass. The Three became silent. Eve looked up at her grandmother giving her a cold stare. China's heart pounded into overtime knowing that she made a mistake.

"You done fucked up now," Day expressed jumping off the table, landing onto his feet growling like a lion.

"I tell you what. If you take us to Mc Donalds right now, I'll forget that you just did that… If not, I'll pull a rabbit out of my hat and it'll be ugly. It's up to you," said Eve, pushing the envelope with China. Eve folded her arms across her chest waiting for an answer.

"Okay, come on, let me get my car keys," China replied, copping deuces with her grand kids. She realized that taking them to McDonalds, will be a lot more easier to cope with, than going to war with these two. China goes into her room to get the car keys. "Are you guys ready?"

"Yeah," they replied in unison, like some obedient

children. They threw the rolling pin and wooden spoon on the couch and exited the house, getting inside China's vehicle. China puts her 9mm in her right pocket and covers it with her white long sleeve T-shirt, as she climbed into the car and smashed down Avalon boulevard, in route to McDonalds.

*****

Tina-Ru pushes east down Rosecrans Blvd to the hood, in her black super sport Monte Carlo, on gold and chrome Dayton rims. She pulls to the corner of Rosecrans, about to make a right turn onto Avalon Blvd. Due to heavy traffic, she gets stuck at the corner. Her trunk is rattling from the 12 inch, woofers and thousand watt amp, pounding *Children's story* by Slick Rick. She sees a break in traffic and mashes off. Not paying attention, looking in the opposite direction, towards the bus stop, hoping that she can catch somebody slipping. She bangs and scrapes her front right rim against the curb, causing sparks. She quickly stops in front of the 76-

gas station, hoping the damage is not too severe. She jumps out to examine. The rim is in pretty bad shape. If she drives, it can become worse. She turns her hazard lights on, jumps out and blazes up a Newport.

"Fuck!" Tina-Ru shouted, looking at her banged up Dayton rim. She glances at her watch pissed, blowing smoke through her nose.

"Aha! ...That's what you get you punk ass slob bitch!" yelled a car load of men driving south on Avalon boulevard, in a blue four door, 86 Chevy Caprice Classic. "Fuck slobs, cuzz!"

Tina-Ru flipped the car load of Crips the bird. She motioned for them to turn around, but they wasn't that foolish. Where she is standing is heavily populated with Pirus. Plus, inside of her car she's strapped with a Glock 9mm. "I bet you won't turn around coward! Fuck crabs!"

*****

China slowly pulls away from the drive through

window, two happy meals later. Her grandkids are not saying a word, due to stuffing their face. China felt like she won the war with these two knuckle head muthafucka's. She smiles proudly as she speeds west on Rosecrans Boulevard, in route to the house. She makes a right onto Avalon Boulevard, noticing a stranded Tina-Ru and pulls over to aid and assist her Piru comrade. Tina is happy that her big homie just happened to be out and about.

"Blood, what happened?" asked China, as she strolls toward Tina-Ru, blazing up a cigarette.

"I was turning on Avalon, not looking and banked my shit against the curb, then scraped it. I'm hella mad blood," Tina explained, thumping the remainder of her cigarette into the street. A tow truck slows down by the two vehicles. "Hey, I need for you to tow my shit, blood!" The truck pulls over and assist Tina-Ru.

"Blood, bring your shit to my house. We can fix it over there," said China, taking one long drag from the cigarette, before disposing it into the street.

Fifteen minutes later, Tina's vehicle is at the mercy of the tow truck. "Okay, do you guys want me to follow you?" asked the Hispanic man.

"Yeah, we're not going far. I live right off of Avalon on 129th street," China explained, as her and Tina climbed into the car.

"Okay, I'll follow you ma'am," replied the tow truck man, eager to get paid for his services.

"Hi, niece and nephew. How are you doing?" asked Tina-Ru, looking in the backseat at Eve and Day, who are quietly eating French fries minding their own business. They both flip Tina-Ru the bird.

"Don't get them started, please. You already know how they get," China demanded, looking at her grandkids through the rearview mirror. They quietly continue to eat, with birds still flipped at their granny. China smiles at the two future Pirus as she pushes down

Avalon Blvd. Five minutes later, China pulls all the way into her driveway, parking her vehicle in front of the garage, in the backyard. Tina, China and her grandkids exit the vehicle. China takes her grandkids inside the house, through the backdoor. Tina-Ru walks through the driveway, until she reaches the front gate, motioning for the tow truck to bring her car at this particular spot. The tow truck places Tina-Ru's Monte Carlo in the driveway successfully. China comes out of the front door smoking a cigarette, in the front yard.

After the Hispanic disconnects the vehicle, Tina-ru hands him a crispy fifty dollar bill. The Hispanic man walks off thanking the two for his pay and nice tip Tina gave him. He leaves the scene.

Smurf, Vanity and Kay Kay pulls up in a candy apple red K-5 blazer, on all gold Daytons, pounding 'Tonite," by D.J. Quik. They pull the truck over and join their two homegirls inside the yard.

"Blood, what happened to your shit?" asked

Smurf, walking up to the damaged vehicle, kicking the tire.

"I cracked my shit on the corner of Rosecrans and Avalon," Tina replied, rolling her eyes at the thought.

"How did you do that, blood?" Vanity asked.

"Not looking, was eyeing the bus stop across the street, to see if I can catch someone slipping," Tina responded, laughing at the thought.

"Blood can fix your shit in Gardena. My shit was bent up like that. And he don't charge no way out ass price neither," Kay Kay explained, examining the Dayton wire rims.

As they were all in the yard conversating, Solomon and Christina pulls in front of the house in Christina's 500 SL Mercedes Benz. Their conversation stops, and everyone focuses on Solo and his baby mama as they come over to pick up Day and Eve, knowing that their grandmother would be more than happy to release them muthafuckers.

Solomon jumps out of the driver's side of the vehicle, dressed in a black long sleeve, button down Guess shirt and matching jeans, with the camel beige Walla-bees on. He walks around to the passenger's side to let Christina out, who is dressed to the nines, shitting on everything around her. Her curvaceous frame hugged every stitch, of the black body dress that she was wearing; complimenting her four inch Moschino suede boots that came to her knees and flat ironed hair, that hung down her back. They acknowledged everyone in the yard, as they walked to the front going inside. China follows behind.

Tina-Ru quickly gets an attitude seeing their school teacher and ex-lover go inside of China's residence. It was one thing to be at their residence and be obedient, but it was another thing for them to come to the hood, looking like movie stars. Tina-Ru is contemplating showing her ass for some attention.

Sabrina steps out of her grandmother's house across the street, in red clothing from head to toe and post up on the porch.

Deena and Jimbo pulls up in a black 1983 coupe de ville on daytons and vouges. Deena kisses her lover in the mouth, before exiting his vehicle, with her work uniform on. He gets in the wind. She sees that everyone is in China's yard she decides to hand out also. "Blood, what's good?" she asked the crowd, talking to no one in particular.

"Shit, just hanging. I banked my shit on the curb blood," Tina-Ru explained rubbing her chin.

Deena looks at the damaged rim. "Take it over there to that shop on Western in Gardena."

"That's what I said, dude will hook you up for a little bit of nothing," Kay Kay added.

"Your super star brother is in y'all moms house, with his baby momma," Tina-Ru spat, with larceny in her heart.

Deena had a look of confusion on her face, wondering why Tina had an attitude. "Is that right?" *Let it go bitch!*

Deena-Ru, what's up wit it blood?" asked Smurf, laughing at Tina-Ru and her shenanigans.

"Aw shit, you know. Just trying to make this shit make sense," Deena responded, shaking her head out of disappointment. "Vanity, Kay Kay, what's up with ya'll homie?"

"Aint shit blood just hanging. Trying to stay above water that's all," Vanity replied, placing a red tie around her braided ponytail.

"I guess the peace treaty is officially over with huh?" asked Kay Kay, who is a little disappointed.

"Oh yeah, that shit is over with. I just got banged on by some crabs in a flue (blue) Caprice," Tina-Ru explained, laughing. She was hoping they would've been foolish enough, to turn around to get popped on. Especially, the mood that she was in at the time.

"It's not over with in Watts. They still trucing. So if you wanna mix and mingle with cats from the other side, you have to go to the Nickersons, Jordan Downs, or the Imperial Courts," Smurf explained, giving up to date and accurate information.

"I got me a lil Crip boy toy from U.G.C. (Underground Crips) that's my nigga," Deena replied, smiling. "That's who dropped me off a minute ago."

Smurf began chuckling. "I think everybody fucked with someone from the other side. That's what made this whole shit fun. I was fucking with this nigga from Shotgun."

"Shit, I ain't go lie. I had a nigga from Grape Street and a bitch from school yard," Vanity responded giggling.

"I kept it on the red team. I didn't fuck with no rip

niggas," Kay Kay added, curling her lip at the traitors.

"Shit, bitch you don't know what you're missing. Them Crip niggas go," Vanity shot back clowning, giving Deena and Smurf some dap.

Nine hit the block, coming from Towne Avenue, in his electronic wheelchair. He pulls up to the front gate and acknowledges everyone's presence. Out of nowhere the sheriff pulls up with force, and jumps out on Nine. It's Officer Milano and a female officer named Hoffman.

"Don't move wise guy," Milano ordered, walking up on Nine with his hand on his pistol, but it's not drawn. "Put your hands on top of your head."

"What did I do? You guys know that I cannot walk," Nine express, placing his hands on top of his head, with an attitude.

"You're a known gang member from this area, and a threat to this community," Milano replied, fucking with Nine for no reason at all. He's looking for some get back from that shooting up at Enterprise Park that night. He walks up to nine and shakes him down.

"Ain't that a bitch...I grew up around here, I'm from this neighborhood," Nine responded heated. He knows Milano is on some bullshit right now.

Smurf walked to the driveway and closed the gate, then walked over and secured the front entrance gate, so that the pigs wouldn't step into the yard.

"Um, I'm gonna ask you ladies to step out of the yard, so that I could shake you guys down for weapons," ordered the female officer, trying to call their bluff.

"Bitch, you must be a rookie. Why would I step off of my property, onto the public sidewalk so that you can grope me?" Deena asked, knowing her rights. "All of us are in my yard, minding our fucking business."

Eve and Day bursted through China's front bar door furious, in route to help their Uncle Nine. "Uncle Nine! Uncle Nine! Are you okay?"

Nine turns to the right noticing Eve and Day. "Yeah, I'm okay. Uncle Nine is good. Y'all make sure that y'all stay inside the gate. Don't come out the yard, okay? Do that for Uncle Nine, stay in the yard I'm okay," he pleaded with his nephew and niece.

"Okay, Uncle Nine, we're gonna stay inside the yard," Day replied respectfully. They have a few choice words for the cops, if Uncle Nine gives the word.

Officer Hoffman squats down spread eagle in front of the gate, facing the twins. "Oh, how sweet, you guys are twins … what is your names?"

"What's that?" asked Day, pointing at Officer Hoffman pussy lips, that are protruding through her pants.

"What's what honey?" Hoffman asked, looking at the direction that his finger is pointing causing her to look at her own pussy. She plays it off and points at the ground smiling. "Are you talking about right here?"

"No," Day shot back. He walked up on the gate and pointed his little finger through the gates hole and pointed right at her pussy. "Right there...What's that?"

Everyone in the yard cracks up laughing, you never know what these two demons have up their sleeve.

Milano listens to the two zebra kids make fun of his partner. *I wonder are those Christina kids. Little smart monkeys.*

"That's not appropriate for kids," Hoffman responded embarrassed, she stands up after the two don't feed into her game.

Christina comes out into the front yard to grab the twins. She sees her ex-husband but gives him no attention. "Eve and Day, come her please." They both run to her grabbing both of her legs.

Officer Milano stops frisking Nine and walks up to the gate, to get a closer look at his ex-wife, who is looking like something to eat. "Christina."

Nine slides to the driveway entrance of the gate, Deena lets him in and secures it. Officer Hoffman walks up to the gate, standing beside her partner. She's in the blind to what's really going on.

Christina turns to her ex, with a look of disgust on her face. "Yes."

"May I have a word with you? Please. Milano pleaded, he couldn't stand to see no one else with Christina and the thought of some spear chucker getting her pregnant, was a devastating blow to his ego.

"Yes, as long as my fiancé is present," Christina shot back in a sassy tone, pissing him off even more.

As on cue, Solomon walks out of his mother's home, with China trailing behind. He stands next to Christina, frowning at Officer Milano. China stands next to her son grilling both officers.

"Hey, I know you, you the co-star on L.A.P.D.

Blues," said Hoffman, not knowing what's really going on. She looks around and instantly feels the tension in the air getting thicker by the second.

"I would like to speak with you in private Christina," Milano asked again, forming a lump in his throat.

"You and I have nothing to talk about. I'm sorry," Christina responded, grabbing Eve and Day by the hand and walking them back into the house.

"Fuck the Police! My mama don't wanna talk to you!" Day shouted, from the top of his lungs, as Christina took them back inside and closed the door shut behind her.

"I take it that you know these people." Hoffman asked, in a low tone trying to go unnoticed.

"Yes, that's my ex-wife." Milano responded, soon after bursted into tears. Hoffman consoled him.

China nipples, hardened from the sight of this pig

crying. She wished nothing but death for Milano, for what he did to Chinadog. She looks on.

Officer Milano felt defeated, worthless and played all at the same time.

"Okay, ladies and gentlemen. I'm going to ask you guys to go inside, please," said Officer Hoffman, going too far because she has a gun and a badge.

"Bitch please. You're the police, not the National Guard," China vented, giving the female hard looks. "You're going a little too far. We don't give a fuck about him crying. On Piru Blood."

"Have a little compassion for someone who's having a bad day," Hoffman shot back, not knowing her partners history with this family.

"Are you fucking serious right now lady cop?" China asked, firing up a Newport in between her lips. "We have history with this officer."

Hoffman looks at Milano, whose face is streaming

tears down on both sides of his cheeks, weeping. With the swiftness, Officer Milano takes his handgun, sticks it in his mouth and pulls the trigger. The bullet came out of the back of his head. His lifeless corpse slammed onto the pavement, motionless. Officer Hoffman began panicking, as she called for a paramedic and more officers. The street was blocked off with yellow tape immediately.

Smurf, Kay Kay, and Vanity sped walked through the driveway gate, jumped back into the truck and sped off down 129th street, disappearing in traffic. Nine wheeled himself through the gate and away from China's residence with the quickness. Deena simply walked across the street, where her sister was already posted. They both went inside. Christina rushed from the house with the kids, Solomon trails behind, as they all load into the Mercedes and sped off into traffic.

Two patrol cars zoomed down 129th street stopping in front of China's residence. China fired up a cigarette and walked back into the house smiling like a kid on Christmas day, with a tree full of presents. Tina-Ru looks on stunned, as she lights up another cigarette and shoves it into her mouth, puffing out of sheer nervousness and disbelief.

Hoffman explains to the arriving officers of what had taken place. Officers just stood over him not touching him. The paramedics arrived, they see that it's no way of bringing him back, they call the coroners. Every news channel in Los Angeles arrives to the scene in a matter of ten minutes. T.V. shows interrupted with a news flash, at what had just happened. The block was filled with neighbors and onlookers, who were glad that Milano had taken his own life. No one that knew him considered him a good cop, or a cop who came to serve and protect the neighborhood. A hundred and twenty ninth street, is now one of the most popular streets in Los Angeles County, due to this self-inflicted act.

Tina-Ru walks inside China's residence and watch

all the fuckery take place, through the living room window.

"Man, this was one hell of a day. Never in a hundred years, did I think that I would see some shit like that. That was a funky cold medina. But it was necessary, fuck em and feed em fish," China explained, happy about the stunt that he pulled. Now she doesn't have to get her hands dirty.

Tina-Ru is still in disbelief of what Milano had done to himself. But at the same time she's happy, she no longer has to deal with his shenanigans or his freaky behavior. "Yeah, I guess it's true. Every dog does have his day."

Milano's corpse laid on the concrete for over two hours, covered in a blood stained sheet, before the meat wagon scraped him up. Now the Pirus that heard about this necessary act, feels like the score is even with them and the sheriff. Later that night, news cameras and police officers from all over L.A. county, had a vigil right in front of China's residence. Piru gang members watched the ceremony from a distance snickering, occasionally verbally disrespecting Milano's legacy. Once the ceremony was over, gang members took the candles and hurled them at ongoing traffic on El Segundo Blvd; then wrote 'Fuck the Police,' on the sidewalk and nearby walls, letting everyone know their feelings towards the police. The next day, news channels aired the act on the news, sending the Pirus reputation amongst the elite bangers in Los Angeles. The saga continues.

FOURTEEN

March 10, 1993   Monday 5:00 p.m.

Solomon and Ty-Stick gave birth to Nadu, a newborn baby girl that weighed 6 lbs. and six ounces. Ty-Stick moved inside of Solomon's Inglewood home three months ago and has been living there ever since. She's on the same kind of schedule that Sara is on, except he sees Ty-Stick more often, because she is employed by him as a personal assistant and his emergency pussy in the glass.

Ty-Stick before the pregnancy was already thick, now that she dropped the baby she is thick in all the right places. They both lie in the bed watching *'Which way is up,'* enjoying each other's company. The baby is in the crib sound asleep.

"How is your family doing, since that one-time (police) blew his head off in front of your house?" Ty-Stick asked braiding her hair into one long ponytail.

"Man, I was in the front yard when he did that. I mean shit, everybody is glad. That fool killed my step father, dropping him off in Front Hood," Solomon explained rubbing his chin, replaying the actual event in his head again.

"Oh, I feel you. Trust me, I feel you on that. I had a few homies that got killed by Lennox Sheriff in our hood and they ain't nothing nice," Ty-Stick expressed, rolling her eyes at the thought.

"I don't' know, I don't be in the hood like that anymore. I have too much to lose. I don't wanna throw my acting career out the window fucking with the police. That'll be going backwards, on everything," Solomon explained seriously.

"And I don't want you to either baby," Ty-Stick replied, pecking Solomon on the lips. Solomon seemed a little puzzled. Ty-Stick noticed his facial expression. "What's wrong baby?"

"I'm still tripping off one of my homegirls. I seen

her get dropped off by the police, the night of my birthday party," said Solomon, shaking his head thinking about it.

"What? Get dropped off by the police? asked a shocked Ty-Stick.

"Yeah, but it was the one that killed himself," said Solomon.

"What? You still don't trust her?" asked Ty-Stick out of concern.

Solomon shook his head. "Nawh, I still don't trust her....I wonder what they had going?"

Ty-Stick couldn't answer that one, she just shook her head, hunching her shoulders. "She from your set?"

"Yeah, My homegirl Tina-Ru?"

"I was in Central (Juvenile hall) with her. She looks like Kim Fields," Ty-Stick expressed. "She was down though. She whooped some bitch from Compton Crip ass."

"That's her," Solomon responded, nodding agreement.

"You want that head put to bed?" ty-stick asked, getting serious.

*****

Bitch, you screwed up big time. Don't think just because my partner committed suicide, you were getting off the hook that easy. Now, you're under my care and I run a much tighter ship than Milano," Esson explained, ramming his penis into her mouth with force, causing Tina to choke and gag. "Am I making myself clear?"

Tina took his swipe out of her mouth. "Yes, I understand."

"I want you to do everything in your power, to help take that womanizer down. He stole my partner's wife and we want revenge. I'm not going to rest, until this mission is accomplished for my partner. I was there.

I helped Milano kill that son-of-a-bitch Chinadog. Fuck him, who was he?" Esson vented, at the thought of that big black muthafucker.

That was my big homie! "I hear you. Just give me a little time," Tina-Ru replied, thinking of a master plan. She was going beyond the call of duty, to make Christina's life miserable.

"I'm dedicating this to the memory of my partner," Esson replied, in a firm tone, grabbing Tina by the ears and fucking her face with force.

FIFTEEN

March 15, 1993   Friday 3:00 p.m.

"Listen up, I want you two guys on your best behavior today, okay?" Solomon demanded, pointing his finger at the two demons. "Your grandfather is coming over to hang out with us. Don't run him off. Do you guys follow me?"

"Yes sir," they both responded in unison, knowing damn well, they're both lying through their damn teeth.

Their conversation was interrupted by the ringing of the doorbell. Solomon strolls to the front door and opens it. "Hey pops, how you doing? Come inside." Robert steps in giving his son a half hug, being that his other hand is full of gifts for his grandkids. Solomon notices the cage. They sit inside the living room. "What you got there?"

"A puppy," Robert responded proudly. "I brought my grandkids a puppy."

Eve and Day rushed over to their grandfather, when they heard the word gift. Robert placed the cage onto the floor and opened the cage. Out came a blue nose baby pit bull. Eve and Day instantly roughed him up, causing the puppy to growl and bite at them. The two were pumped.

"What are you guys going to name the puppy?" Solomon asked, knowing that it's going to be something off the wall.

They both paused at the question in deep thought, thinking of a name.

"Let's name him Damu," said Eve, grabbing onto the dogs tail.

"Damu? No, this is a blue nose female pit-bull. Let's name her Smurf," Day looked at Eve in awe, forming a devilish smirk on his face.

"Thank-you for the puppy grand pappy," said Eve.

"Yeah, thanks grandpa," Day responded, walking

up to his leg and hugging it. The puppy runs down the hallway Eve and Day give chase.

"I appreciate you bringing them a puppy. I should have thought about that a long time ago, that'll keep them busy. Now they have somebody they have to look after," Solomon expressed sincerely.

"Oh, it's my pleasure, anything for the grandkids. So, how you been doing?"

"Just staying focused and taking it one day at a time," Solomon responded proudly.

"Yeah, your mother was telling me about that incident that occurred in front of her house, when the officer shot himself in the mouth" Robert stated, shaking his head about the situation. "That's a shame."

"Yeah, it was a shame, but he had it coming. I believe his conscience was eating him up," said Solomon rubbing his chin, thinking about the day that he took his life.

Christina comes inside of their home a little exhausted from running errands all day. Solomon and Robert stand up in preparation of introducing his fiancé to his father. Christina steps all the way into the living room, noticing her uncle. "Uncle Robert?" Christina asked, out of shock and disbelief. They both give each other a long hug.

That's why our kids are so fucked up in the head. We're cousins...Aw shit! "Well, I guess I don't have to introduce you guys to each other." Robert pulls back examining his niece admiring her curvaceous figure. "It's good to see you Christina."

SIXTEEN

April 10, 1993   Wednesday 1:30 pm

Tina-Ru got the front Dayton wire rim fixed on her super sport Monte Carlo. She pulls to the gas pump at the Arco on Rosecrans and Figueroa Street. This gas station is on the borderline most occupants that buys gas from here are Bloods. However, this station is more on the Gardena, Payback Crip Territory side. Tina comes from inside the pay station, putting twenty dollars on pump number five. She removes the gas cap and inserts the gas nozzle, keeping a close eye on all the incoming and outgoing traffic in the gas station. Two farts later, the gas stops. She returns the nozzle and gas cap back to their designated areas. She jumps in the vehicle and mash out, north on Figueroa Street. As she reaches the stop light on 135th and Figueroa, a brown 1988 minivan pulls to the passenger side of her car. As soon as she looks over to her right, shots rang out from the van riddling her vehicle with bullets. Tina ducks and puts the pedal to the metal, but the car only moved into the intersection, due to the bullets killing the engine. Tina screamed for her mother and Jesus to save her life. Suddenly, the firing stops, and the mini-van speeds off east on 135th street. By the grace of God she was hit, but wasn't dead, but her vehicle is D.O.A (Dead on arrival). Who would wanna take out Tina-Ru, being that Milano is dead?

SEVENTEEN

April 12, 1993   Friday 1:30 a.m.

A brown 1986 Chevy Caprice pulls in front of China's residence, and turns off their lights. Moments later, from the back passenger's window, out comes the barrel of an AK-47, firing numerous shots at her house, collapsing the kitchen and living room windows.

After the shots stopped, the vehicle turned their lights back on. Like a madman, China crept alongside her vehicle in the driveway, and fired numerous rounds into the brown Nova, as it sped off with its back window and passenger's door window missing, due to China getting active. She ran into the middle of the street, while inserting another clip trying to catch up with the vehicle, while firing more rounds at the Nova.

"Mama...Mama, are you okay?" asked Deena, jogging from their grandmother's home, to China's front yard with a loaded 9mm in her right hand.

"Yeah, I'm bool, blood," China shot back pissed, at what just took place. She lights up a cigarette to calm her nerves. "Blood, let's go in the house before One Time comes."

"Yeah, you're right," Deena replied, as they both walked inside of China's residence, kicking back on the couch and recliner chair.

"Blood, it's been hella sneaky shit going on since that pig blew his brains back," said China, calculating all of the events that have been happening lately. She stares into space taking another drag from the cigarette.

"What happened just a minute ago?" Deena asked, trying to put the pieces to the puzzle together.

"I just so happened to get me a glass of water from the kitchen. I see a brown Nova pull up, killing their lights. Something told me to get my strap. As soon as I did, they started busting at the house. I crept out the back door and through the driveway and hollered back at their asses, unloading. I put in another clip and ran behind they ass, Bitch muthafuckas!" China explained, as she disposed the cigarette inside of the ashtray on the coffee table.

Deena starts laughing. "You had to come out of retirement, huh blood?"

"On Piru," China shot back. She walks over to the living room's light switch and shuts it off. Then does the same in the kitchen. A patrol car pulls up in front of China's home, shining the spotlight on the house examining the various bullet holes, above and around the window. China and Deena become quiet, as they bob and weave the cop's shining light. Their ass-holes tightens out of fear, praying that the police don't come to the front door asking questions. After five minutes of faking like they really came to serve and protect. More shots rang out on 132nd Street. The patrol car sped off to investigate.

"Blood, did you hear them shots just now?" asked Deena, becoming hyper of all the gun play. Her nipples hardened, she's ready to bust her gun.

"Yeah, I told you hella strange shit has been happening blood, on Piru," China responded confused, still trying to make some sense of all this.

Deena jumps onto her feet excited. "Blood, let's jump in your car and go C-Kaying (Crip killing).

"Hell nawh, bitch you tripping. It's so many police out there, you wouldn't make it past San Pedro Street. You're asking to go to prison. I'm bool blood. I have to get these windows fixed, first thing in the morning," said China, making a whole lot of sense. She'll be damned if she has to sit up in the county jail, for not making wise choices. After sitting up in jail for days and weeks at a time, the walls had started talking to China, in a conversation that she's not trying to converse with on a second go around. "Why don't you go in the house and lay low, before you get yourself caught up for not thinking."

Deena stood onto her feet. "Yeah, I guess you're

right. Because I would sure as hell be pissed at myself, for not taking your advice sitting in the county, fighting over the bottom bunk."

"I'm trying to tell you," China agreed, not even trying to replay that scenario in her head again.

"Alright blood," said Deena, as she walked back to her grandmother's home across the street."

"Alright," China replied, going back to her bedroom, to go to sleep.

*****

Nine is hanging in his driveway, dressed in red from head to toe, hanging with his Piru comrades. Every member is strapped, due to all the anonymous shootings in the last couple of days. On top of that, the sheriff is still pissed about their partner Milano, committing suicide and the Pirus disrespecting his vigil and honor. Pirus make sure that they travel in groups of at least three. This click of Pirus is not under any gang injunction. If so, under law they would not be able to hang in groups of three or more. Every gang member is cautious as to how they move, because of this law.

For some strange reason, every time the police is hot. Marijuana buyers seem to come through the area, looking to purchase some weed, at a back to back pace. Nine and a few of his homies who are out slanging weed are making money today hand over fist. Nobody's complaining, but the police. A grey crown vic slides past the group of Pirus. Everyone eyed the vehicle closely, not sure if the vehicle were police, Jackers or Crips.

Nine took the blunt from his ear and blazed it up. "Has anybody been up to Killer King to bee (see) Tina-Ru?"

"She still in I.C.U., she still has a few bullets lodged in her back, chest and lungs," Smurf explained, looking down at the ground becoming sad, for her homegirl. "We'll be able to see her after she has the operation and they remove the bullets."

A black 1988 Jeep Grand Cherokee hits the block, speeding and swerving out of control. The noise startled everyone, causing the Pirus to clutch their weapons and stand behind vehicles, using them as shields.

"Blood, my nerves are bad. All this anticipating got me ready to shoot something, or somebody," Nine expressed, heated at the thought. He removes his nine from his pocket and places it on his lap. The sheriff hits the block, Nine shoves his pistol underneath his wheel chair seat cushion, and warn others. "One Time blood!" Everyone that was strapped, walked all the way into the driveway, by the backyard.

"Everybody run blood, here comes One Time!" yelled Officer Truman, sarcastically, sticking his head out of the patrol car, as it slowed down in front of Nine's residence. He looks at Nine smirking. "What's up Nueve? Killed any crabs or Mexican cartel affiliates for financial gain lately?" Truman knew his background.

Nine shook his head with a look of disgust on his

face. "Nah, not lately. Why?"

"Because your name has not been on our radar. Either you became a smarter killer, or you went into retirement," Truman replied, trying to use the Jedi mind trick for information.

"Man, I'm not in the game no more. I can't even walk. What can I do?" Nine responded, not feeding into his bullshit.

"You can call shots from your wheelchair," Truman replied, he can see that Nine is a little jittery and decided to fuck with him. He slowly opens the door to his patrol car. "What are my chances of me getting out of this vehicle, shaking you down and finding a pistol and some weed?"

Nine eyes widens out of fear, letting a silent one escape from his keister, before he spoke. "Slim and none. I don't hustle or tote pistols anymore."

"Yeah, right and I'm a unicorn with biker shorts

on," Truman responded sarcastically, walking up on Nine, scaring the shit out of him.

Knock! Knock! Knock!

Out of nowhere, bullets rang out knocking out the front windshield of the police vehicle. Truman runs back to the patrol car, checking on his partner who is okay, but had jumped out the vehicle, with weapon in hand. Truman drew his weapon looking around, radioing for back up.

Knock! Knock! Knock! Knock! Knock!

Both officers ducked behind the doors of their vehicle. Nine, slowly pushed his wheel chair in reverse until he reached his kitchen door. Vanity comes out of the door, he gives her the pistol, she goes back inside, locking the door behind her. Two more patrol cars pulls up to where Truman and his partner are. From a distance, more shots rang out, followed by the sound of a car burning rubber, fleeing the scene from a street nearby. All three cars took off, in route to where they think the shooting came from.

All the gang members ran back to Nine's front yard and driveway, quickly filling it up.

"Damn blood, I wonder who's been doing all this busting around here lately?" Smurf asked, talking to no one in particular.

"Whoever is doing it, thank-you. You saved my ass that time, whew!" Nine expressed, looking up at the clouds with his hands in prayer, thanking God and all the homies looking over after them.

"It's probably the police faking, trying to get us up under that gang injunction. Once we're up under that, we can get locked up for hanging with each other. That shit is so fucking stupid," Kay-Kay said, becoming pissed at the thought.

"I don't think it's the police. But I betcha we know who it is. The police wouldn't damage their own vehicle like that," Nine replied using common sense.

Knock! Knock! Knock! Knock! Knock! Knock!

All the Pirus ducked and ran for cover. Whoever this anonymous person was, fired a high-powered rifle at the gang.

"Blood, whoever it is, they going hard in the paint. On Piru blood," Nine said, wheeling himself behind his truck that's in the driveway. "I don't wanna get killed being nosy."

Within a matter of five minutes, the whole neighborhood from 135th street, to El Segundo Boulevard was congested with patrol cars. The ghetto bird arrived circling the area, in search of the shooter. Police went door to door asking for permission, to search backyards and garages. After thirty minutes of fuckery, the sheriff came up empty handed. Today was a good day.

*****

Since Officer Milano took his own life, Christina

feels like a burden has been lifted off her. But for some strange reason, she still carries her pistol as if her life is in danger. She already made a vow, to protect her and her family no matter what. Today has been one of those, "I'm not in the mood to be fucked with days. She's been running errands all morning and most of the afternoon, getting things on her agenda accomplished. By Solomon watching the kids when she do run her errands, makes her day much smoother and stress free.

Christina pushes her 500 SL onto the on ramp of the riverside freeway, heading north. As she blends through traffic, she notices a Hispanic man wearing a hat with dark shades on, trailing her in a black 454 super sport truck. Every time she switches to a different lane, he does the same. Christina reaches into her purse and pulls out her 9mm and places it onto her lap. She drives for several miles with the truck still trailing behind her. She reaches the on ramp that connects her to the Harbor freeway and gets on, so does the truck. As they reach the city of Lomita, the 454ss speeds past Christina and gets directly in front of her vehicle. She thought that was a little strange. She looks into the rear-view mirror and notices two men behind her in a green and black GMC Syklone truck, wearing shades. Christina's heart rate goes up a notch. Like a skilled race car driver, Christina speeds up and switches over to the next lane, to her right and rolls down both windows. Christina doesn't believe in violence, but at the same time, she doesn't believe in being a victim either. She speeds past the 454ss and gets into the far left lane and passes the speed limit by five miles. She drives with no problems for several miles.

The truck revs up the engine and tries to go around Christina's Benz but she speeds up also, making it impossible. They race side by side for a half a mile. Christina looks around for the police and Highway Patrol. The man in the 454ss, looks over into his passenger's seat, grabbing something while rolling down his window.

Out of nervousness, Christina ups her 9mm and squeezes three hot-balls at his face. The truck slams on its brakes causing pandemonium. The GMC Syklone speeds up, trying to get around the black 500sl Benz, but Christina doesn't allow it. She notices the freeway sign, El Segundo Blvd ½ mile. She speeds up and gets off on El Segundo Boulevard making a right turn studying her doors rear view mirror. She gets caught at the stoplight on Figueroa and El Segundo, in the turning lane. Like the boogeyman in a scary movie, both trucks speed off the off ramp and gets directly behind her. She got a break in the traffic, making a left turn speeding north on Figueroa Blvd, both trucks get caught in the traffic but muscled their way through, speeding after her. She notices the vehicles in her rear-view mirror.

Both trucks flicked their lights off and on, knowing that they're being watched by her. Once they saw that she wasn't slowing down for that move, they both began wailing their horns at her. Christina still refused to stop, both trucks pulled over once they reached 121st street. Christina kept pushing, jumping back onto the Harbor freeway heading north, in route to her home with her family.

EIGHTEEN

April 19, 1993   Friday 12:15 p.m.

What started off on the good foot as an experimental project, is now turning into a don't get caught slippin' relationship. Deena has been doing the right thing, going to work and coming straight home to her man cooking, cleaning and freaking. On top of that, she even breaks bread with Jimbo when she gets her check. Those actions alone has been going to Jimbo's head. He's been doing too much, like he's a pimp or something and Deena is his whore. He's been caught twice, with two different hoes on two different occasions, and both bitches were Crips. Deena came to blows with one of them for constantly cussing her. After asking her respectfully to stop the verbal abuse, Deena took off on her beating her down something terrible. Jimbo had to pull Deena off his Crip comrade.

Now their relationship is at the level where he is

now starting to put his hands on Deena, something that she's not going to tolerate. They had a fight last week, when Jimbo slapped her, because he was in the wrong. Deena gave him a warning and told him that he doesn't want to meet Deena-ru, because she is a Crip killer with three hot ones up under her belt to prove it.

He laughed it off like Deena was faking with the murder game. She did all that she could do to not go that route, but like most hardheaded people, he has to learn the hard way.

Jimbo and Deena pushes up Figueroa Street in route to drop her off. They just came from the Roadium drive in seeing two different movies, in which they were unable to see, due to them arguing, fussing and fighting.

"I think after tonight, we should call it quits. All we've been doing lately is fighting and that ain't cool. It's not healthy," Deena expressed, hoping that he would meet her halfway through out this ordeal.

Jimbo rotated the wooden toothpick in his mouth,

from one side to the other, like he's a player. He contemplated on her statement, but refused to reply right away. "You don't decide when it's over for us, I do."

"So, with that being said. I guess you're not trying to break up. I don't want you to get me confused with your Crip home girls. I'm not going for it. You're not going to be disrespecting me every time you're wrong or when one of them punk bitches make you upset and you try to take it out on me," Deena explained, letting it be known that she ain't the one.

"Cuz you tripping!" Jimbo flashed, leaning up against the doors window, staining it up with jerri curl activator. He turns up the volume on his cd changer bumping the chronic, flashing gang signs as he raps along with the song.

Deena nods her head in agreement with her inner-self and came to the conclusion to give Jimbo a dirt nap. When *Nuthin but a G thang* came on, Deena played it off by snapping her fingers and singing along with the song. They finally reach 135th street making a right turn heading east. Deena knows that if she is going to make her move, this is the street to do it on, being that it is surrounded by factories. Deena slowly removes her glock from the right side of her waistline and keeps her right hand in between the door and seat. She slowly reaches over and cock it, Jimbo is still oblivious to what's going on. The car finally gets caught at the red light on 135th and Main. Deena checks her rearview mirror, not a soul in sight. Jimbo looks out of his window, then sees a flash. Deena fed him one to the side of his head and another one in the neck. The force from the bullet, caused his foot to slip off the brake slumping his torso against the window, covering most of it with brain matter. Deena quickly grabbed the steering wheel with her left hand, then stuck her left foot on the gas pedal and drove across Main street, pulling over at the nearest available parking space. The inside reeked of burnt flesh and hair activator. Deena rubbed everything that she think she touched, with her coat before exiting the vehicle. She exited the vehicle unnoticed, hopping the fence at Vanguard Jr. High School, dashing across the playing field, in route to the house which was on the other side of the school.

NINETEEN

April 21, 1993   Sunday 12:31 p.m.

China woke up from a power nap energized. She fires up a Newport and places it in between her lips pulling, trying to get her nicotine fix. She walks into the living room, turning on the stereo, playing Ice Cube's *Amerikkka's Most Wanted* CD. She glances outside through her locked bar door, for anything unusual, due to all the latest fuckery that has been going on.

Smurf pulls to the curbside in a Dodge minivan rental car and jumps out heading to China's front door. China steps out into the front yard, not before grabbing her 9mm out the kitchen cabinet, to meet her young homie.

"Young Smurf, what's good blood?" asked China, as she thumped the remainder of cigarette into the grass, putting her pistol on her waist, behind her. She extends her hand out, Smurf accepts her invite by interlocking P's with her.

"Ain't shit, just doing my rounds checking on you. You straight big homie?" Smurf asked, adjusting her handgun up under her sweatshirt.

"Yeah, I can't complain. About a week ago somebody came through and knocked on my house. I had to get a new window put in. Look, all above the window at them bullet holes, somebody had a chopper," China explained, pointing at the various bullet holes up and around her front window.

Smurf steps up to the window to get a closer look. "Damn, them fools came through chopping, on Piru blood. It's been hella shit going on around here lately. Saturday morning they found a crab nigga dead in his car. They found him on 135th and Main, behind Vanguard stanking. Maybe the fives caught him slipping, I drove past there when I heard about it. That Cadillac looked familiar, but I can't remember where I seen that lac at before."

No sooner than she completed her statement, Deena jogs from across the street into her mother's front yard in a good mood. "What's good love ones?"

China looks at her daughter's body language. She can tell that something is up or she has been a part of something phenomenal. "Why you so damn happy heifer?"

Now Smurf remembers the Cadillac. *Oh, that must have been Deena's work! She caught that nigga straight slipping on Piru!* Smurf thought to herself smiling.

"Aw, ain't shit, just glad to see everybody hanging that's all, "Deena responded smiling, as she adjusted her pistol up under her long sleeve Guess shirt.

"Yeah right, you can tell that bullshit to someone else. I know you," China replied firing up another cigarette, blowing out several smoke rings into the air.

"Smurf what's good homie?"

"Aw blood, I'm good. Just doing my rounds

through the neighborhood, making sure everybody's good," Smurf replied, folding her arms across her chest. "You know they found some nigga dead on 135th and Main, stanking inside of his car."

Deena playfully looked at her fingernails blowing on them, soon after rubbed them onto her shirt, signifying that was her work. China and Smurf grew smirks on their faces already knowing the business. Deena shrugs her shoulders. "Hey, what can I say? I always give niggas the benefit of the doubt."

China and Smurf both give Deena some dap, nodding their head in approval. Deena's reputation is starting to soar. "You've been putting it down I see."

"I'm two ahead of you," Deena boasted to her mother, who was counting each homicide on her fingers. "I'm the reason why you're standing here now, don't forget that," Deena added, winking her eye at her mother.

"Thank-you," China responded, rolling her eyes

out of jealousy.

"Well, on that note, we're all going to bell up to the hospital tonight to holler at Tina-ru. She's out of I.C.U. (Intensive Care Unit) and can now have visits. We're gonna go around six thirty," said Smurf.

"Okay, we'll be up there to kick it with her," Deena replied, as she exits the front yard in route to her granny's house. "I'll holla at y'all tonight blood. Be safe."

"Alright," China and Smurf replied in unison.

*****

Tina-Ru sits up in the bed all teeth, happy that all of her homies are present. Ain't nothing like hood support in the time of need. Tina has lost a few pounds. One of the bullets fragment touched her spine. She's gonna be able to walk again, but with a slight limp. However, if she constantly exercise her spine, by doing hyperextensions, she could possibly have a full recovery and walk normal again. Officer Truman and an investigator came by earlier, interrogating her trying to get some information out of her. Tina was uncooperative.

Her room is filled with red balloons, red bandanas, and stuffed animals dressed in red clothing. Tina is in her room alone, so her visitors are past the recommended amount taking up space and occupancy throughout the entire room. Nurses complained at first, but went ahead and let the hooligans have their way, so that it wouldn't cause any problems.

Smurf, Kay-Kay, Vanity, Deena, Sabrina, China, Nine, Dirt and Klown were all present. The only one missing is Solomon and that is one person that Tina-Ru would love to see right about now. However, she knows that he's on a whole different level and time schedule than everyone else. It was okay with Tina, she wasn't expecting the whole hood to show up anyway. She was surprised that this many people came, along with her immediate family. She feels blessed and loved all at the same time. Everyone's been here since visitation started, which was around 3:00 p.m. Tina has been dosing off, due to being up all day. It is now 7:30 p.m. and visits are over in thirty minutes. The gang decides to let her get some rest.

"Tina blood, we gonna let you rest up homie. We bee (see) you over there nodding like a dope fiend," Nine said clowning, as he rolled his wheelchair up to her bed.

"Okay, homies, come back tomorrow and bring me some trail mix," Tina responded, laughing, as she nodded off again.

All the Pirus left Tina's room respectfully, not causing any problems on the way out the door. Tina fell into a deep sleep, due to the strength of the medicine that she took. She counted sheeps, ducks and dollar signs for hours uninterrupted.

Tina was awakened by an open hand slap that landed on the right side of her face, heating her face up like an electric blanket.

Tina opened her eyes horrified, at what had just happened. A squirt of piss escaped from her pussy, from the unexpected assault on her face. She tried to reach for the emergency button to get some assistance, but was a day late and a dollar short, due to her assailant already removing it, before they stepped in to do their dirt. They took the red bandana off the stuffed animal and shoved it into Tina's mouth.

"You faggot ass bitch. You think you're untouchable? Huh, answer me you punk rock bitch," she asked covering her mouth, muzzling her cries and screams. Tina got a chance to see her killer face to face. This woman refused to wear a mask, cause she has plans on killing Tina, who had a look of confusion written all over her face, as to why her. Tina tried to say something, but was cut short by the smacking on the left side of her face. "Bitch, stay away from my baby daddy. He ain't fucking with you and now that you seen my face, I'm killing your punk ass."

Tina tried to swing once her life depended on it, but was unsuccessful. The female went inside of her pocket, pulling out a bottle of Visine squeezing several drops into both nostrils. Her killer then punched her until she was unconscious. Once there was no movement from Tina, several more drops went into her nose until she coughed. The killer then stuffed the red bandana into Tina's mouth, as she choked her with her hands around her neck applying pressure, until she farted and stopped breathing. The killer kept squeezing until Tina was a corpse, which was another two minutes. The killer let go and slipped away into the darkness.

THE END